CHRISTOPHER BURNS

Christopher Burns was born in 1944, and still spends as much time as possible in the Lake District. He has had three novels published: SNAKEWRIST, THE FLINT BED (which was short-listed for the Whitbread Novel of the Year Award in 1989) and THE CONDITION OF ICE. His stories have appeared in the *London Review of Books*, *London Magazine* and the *Critical Quarterly*, in Heinemann's *Best Short Stories* in 1986 and 1988, and in the collection ABOUT THE BODY, published in 1988 and also available from Sceptre. In 1990 he won a Northern Electric Arts Award for his writing.

Christopher Burns is married and has two sons.

Christopher Burns

THE CONDITION OF ICE

First published in Great Britain in 1990 by Martin Secker & Warburg Ltd.

Sceptre edition 1991

Sceptre is an imprint of Hodder and Stoughton Paperbacks, a division of Hodder and Stoughton Ltd.

The characters and situations in this book are entirely imaginary and bear no relation to any real person or actual happenings.

Printed and bound in Great Britain for Hodder and Stoughton Paperbacks, a division of Hodder and Stoughton Ltd., Mill Road, Dunton Green, Sevenoaks, Kent TN13 2YA. (Editorial Office: 47 Bedford Square, London WC1B 3DP) by Clays Ltd, St Ives plc. Photoset by Rowland Phototypesetting Ltd., Bury St Edmunds, Suffolk.

British Library C.I.P.

Burns, Christopher
  Condition of ice.
  I. Title
  823 [F]

  ISBN 0-340-55203-4

To Jessie and Jonah Prince

1

A LONG WAY FROM HERE, IN ANOTHER COUNTRY, A PART OF MY LIFE has been put on display. For just a few francs anyone can look at all there is left of our friendship, and strangers can gaze at the faces that we had more than fifty years ago.

The display case stands in a small museum down a side-street; I visited it for the anniversary. There are several cases arranged around the walls of a long room, beginning in August 1936 and ending just a few years ago. A scale model of the Versücherin stands in the very centre of the museum, its north face illuminated by harsh electric lights. No sun ever shone so directly on that face.

The model has been guillotined at east, west and south so that it resembles a plinth. The north face, or wall, is triangular in shape and virtually sheer. An attempt has been made to reproduce not only its configurations, but also its colour. The base is turf-green, the exposed rocks black or brown, and the ice has been given a dead, whitish colour, like plaster of Paris. A series of labels has been attached to the wall, and broken lines in red and yellow and blue used to indicate the routes that have been used since the first attempt. Here is the cave, the flume, the web and, almost at the summit, the Kirchner ridge.

And yet the model seems without life and without menace. Although topographically exact, it bears as much relation to reality as a waxwork does to its original model.

The display case contains pieces of our old equipment. To modern eyes we must seem like creatures from the dark ages, with our antiquated methods and our woollen clothing. And yet

1

we had been in the vanguard, and prided ourselves on our rapid Alpine-style technique and lobsterclaw crampons. My own crampons have been placed beside my boots, which look just as they had done on the day I gave them to Otto Seematter. The long strips of razored leather droop over the ankles so that they look like odd, spent plants. Here is my iceaxe, recovered after I had abandoned it, and here is the rope, its sliced end unravelling now.

Beside them are Hansi's clothes, donated by his relatives when the museum was first established. His balaclava, his hat, his shirts and jackets and boots all look disturbingly new, and yet they belong to a vanished past.

At the bottom of the cabinet is an open tobacco tin, found at the back of our shelter by a French team who had climbed the wall fifteen years ago. A yellowing piece of paper is spread out beside it. Although the ink has faded it is still possible to read my name, and Jean's, and the height, and the date.

Beside the case is a large photograph printed on a display board. Otto took it just before we began. Hansi and I stand on a small mound of turf and gaze downwards into the camera lens. Jean is standing between us. Beside our images a printed card explains that this is Ernest Tinnion, his wife, and Hansi Kirchner. We all look youthful and attractive; even my face seems to be good-looking in a strange, tense kind of way, and there is no trace of the priggishness I sometimes think I must have possessed.

Of us all, Hansi is the most photogenic. His open, even features show eagerness, self-possession and confidence. But Jean has not photographed well, and the light has angled across her face in such a way that her expression has been effaced by the heavy contrast. On her lips is a smile, but it appears to be forced, and although she is linked to us she nevertheless seems to be apart.

Behind us is the Versücherin, which is little more than an out-of-focus grey blur, and at our feet is the shadow of the mound.

This has been printed a stark black, and we stand at its edge as if at the rim of a dangerous precipice. We pay it no heed, and stare ahead as if we are secure. Only Jean seems quizzical.

More than half a century separates us now, and yet my whole life has been spent in the shadow of that week. Not a day goes by without me thinking of it; who we were, and what happened, are as real to me now as they ever were.

The last part of our journey was by trap. A man with a long feather in his hat stowed our cases and set the horse at a trot. Despite her tiredness Jean was enchanted, and clung to my arm as I talked to the driver and pointed out sights as we headed up the valley. On each side of the road were houses and farms of whitewashed stone, with fretted balconies and shingle roofs and shutters that were pinned open. Some had painted gable-ends, and beside them tobacco and roses had been planted. Apples ripened in orchards, and in the broad floor of the valley there were fields of wheat, flax, maize, with brilliant poppies growing among the crops. A man with a milkcart drawn by a hound had stopped by a waterpump to give the dog a drink and, a mile further on, a solitary horse stood lazily flicking its tail with a ring of fresh bread hung on its pommel. The rider had dismounted and was standing by a roadside shrine, a tiny dovecot with an open front, which was fastened to a beech tree. Further on there were barns with owl-holes cut into their walls in the shape of goblets or axes. Soon we crossed a river by an old roofed bridge that smelled of hot fir. Our exit was framed with darkness, like a cinema screen, and we rode towards it with our jingling and clopping bouncing all around us. When we came out into the sunlight everything seemed bright, apart from a patch of darkness on the mountains to our right. That, I told Jean, was the north wall.

After another twenty minutes we reached the Seematters'

pension. I had stayed there before with Hansi, and Otto remembered me well. Up until a few years ago, Otto had been a guide. Since he had bought the pension he had lost the taut muscularity of the early photographs, but he still gave the impression of strength rather than indulgence. His shirts were never fastened at the top button, and sometimes he bumped into the furniture as if he had not yet grown used to his increased girth. He was delighted to meet us, and bowed to Jean, beaming with pleasure.

Clara, Otto's wife, also came to greet us. 'This is Mrs Tinnion,' I said, with all the self-importance of a new husband. Clara was grey-haired, stockily built, reliable. I was sure that it was she who really made the pension a success. It was not merely that she was ferociously houseproud and an excellent cook, but she was discreet and understanding, like a favourite aunt. I felt guilty because I had lied to her.

Otto took the luggage up to our room. The bedframe was made of polished pine, and on top of it was a thick mattress and a quilted bedspread made of white cotton. A plain crucifix hung on the wall; there was a dressing-table with a small porcelain bowl filled with newly picked flowers; the curtained French windows had been left open, and led out onto a wooden balcony with spectacular views of valley and mountains. Beside the door hung an oleograph of two Victorian climbers scaling a stylised Matterhorn.

Otto placed our cases on the floor, refused a tip when I searched in my pocket for a coin, and left discreetly, like a man leaving honeymooners alone.

Our lovemaking was confident, sweet, tiring. All the time a breeze from the valley lifted the curtain like a sail, sending it in a billow into the room where it relaxed and swelled again.

Clara had arranged for hot baths to be run for us. I lay in mine and thought of how our journey had begun. We had arranged to meet at the railway station, and I had pulled my hat down over my eyes like a nervous man affecting nonchalance, or pretended to read my copy of *Time and Tide*. Until almost the last moment I was not convinced that she would come.

When I returned I found that a bottle of *spumante* had been left for us on a tray, along with two glasses. Jean thought this a charming gesture. I poured us a drink each, and we touched the glasses together. Their click was like the sound of metal on ice. 'It should be champagne,' I said.

'I don't care; it's a lovely gesture.'

We dressed and sat out on the balcony, one storey above the road, and looked down the long scoop of the valley. I tried not to look at the Versücherin. The sun was hot and a bee hummed near the window.

'Are you happy?' I asked.

'You mean have I done the right thing?'

I was surprised that she put it so boldly. Ever since I had met Jean, her diplomacies and uncertainties had been punctuated by moods of unsettling honesty. Still, I did not expect her to rephrase my question so directly.

'If you want,' I said.

'I don't know, Ernest. Perhaps you can tell better than me. Have I?'

I laughed. 'Why, of course,' I said.

She squeezed my hand. 'That's all that matters then, isn't it?'

That night, as we ate our meal, I noticed the other guests constantly glancing at her. We sat on our own in a corner of the tiny dining room. Floor, ceiling, and furniture were of seasoned pine, and the chairs were so thick they were heavy. Antlers and horns had been fixed along the beams, polished brass ornaments arranged along the stone mantelpiece, chintz curtains hung at the windows. To one side of the fireplace was Otto's collection of climbing books and, most valuable of all, his three volumes of press cuttings. Fixed by the door was a combined thermo-meter and barometer and, above that, three photographs of the

Seematters when they were young, handsome, and had the world at their feet.

Jean was cool and demure, and had dressed in the most fashionable English way.

Several times she extended her fingers when holding her glass, as if to show off the wedding-ring. She ate well, and seldom took her eyes off me. It pleased me to have further confirmation that others found her attractive and, perhaps, desirable. I also felt a twinge of uncertain and irrational jealousy.

Jean laced her fingers together, rested her chin on them, and looked at me with clear blue eyes. Her face was still pale from all our travelling. I thought of how our scheming and deception had come to this, and I was full of admiration for her courage. I wanted to take her hands across the table, to tell her that everything would be all right now. But I had a sudden loss of confidence, as if I was unequal to the demands of our affair. It was as if I had been handed a gift that was both delicate and puzzling, and I was mystified as to what I should do next. To disguise my weakness I began to talk about my boyhood among mountains such as these. I was urbane, knowledgeable, with a voice that was a little too loud. It must have seemed that I was exercising a hold on her that was both tenuous and coarse. But she did not complain, even though nothing that I said was new to her, and she did not check me even though I projected my words too much. Instead she remained quiet, and looked at me as if I was the very pivot of her life.

Apart from two Germans, the other guests were all Swiss. The Swiss left early and returned late, tired and exultant over their little expeditions. They were a group of colleagues from an insurance company, holidaying together in the high Alps. They treated us courteously, but never tried to strike up conversations, no doubt believing we wished to be left alone.

The older German was in his early or middle thirties. He had a broken nose which had been set at an angle, giving his thin, otherwise undistinguished face a lopsided look. When he laughed he showed one crooked incisor. His companion was much younger, about twelve or thirteen, and I took them to be father and son, although the family resemblance was not great. The boy had an air of obsession, as if all his emotions, all his thoughts had been funnelled into one zealously cultivated hobby. Often he could be seen with a frown of furious concentration on his face, and he was seldom completely relaxed. The two of them went for long walks together, the older man taking one, sometimes two, of the many cameras he possessed, and the younger carrying a bag full of jars, boxes, nets and traps. At mealtimes the boy talked with a kind of excited monotony about predation, reproduction, parasites and decay. The older man followed these monologues intently. Usually I thought that he was humouring the boy, and often he asked questions which seemed designed to provoke him into even lengthier bouts of explanation and description. They were both naturalists, I guessed, the younger following in the elder's footsteps, absorbed in their collecting tour. They would be indifferent to the doings of ordinary men, I decided, and too involved in the details of accumulation and taxonomy. But the older man sometimes looked at me with a sharp, unblinking eye. If our paths crossed he would smile with a cool restraint, although the boy, locked within his own passion, would neither acknowledge us nor, if possible, even admit that we were there.

After two days we met them at a shop in the town. I had taken Jean there because it was market day. A brass band played around the statue of the armoured horseman, and the streets were full of stalls selling lace, cheese, cooked meats, caged birds, leather, clothing, and sugared cakes. We stopped to look at some highly ornamented pipes, and Jean held my arm tightly and said that perhaps we would become old Swiss together, she with plaits and a dirndl, I with my felt hat, neckerchief, and ridiculously elaborate pipe. 'Never,' I said, because I could not bear to look too far into the future.

We came face to face with the two Germans when they walked out of a shop selling cameras and binoculars. The older man was putting a film into his pocket, and for a few seconds we accidentally barred each other's way. It was impossible not to speak. The man raised his hat while the boy wheeled round and gazed fixedly into the window of the shop he had just left. 'This is an attractive little town,' the man said in English, 'is that not so?'

'It's lovely,' Jean said.

He knew our names because, as he confessed with a disarming smile, he had asked Otto Seematter. His own name was Max Volkwein, and the boy was his nephew Bruno. They were on a short holiday together before Bruno had to return to his school.

'You've been collecting lots of things, Bruno,' Jean said. Max translated for the boy, who replied with a smile which vanished as suddenly as it had appeared.

Max began to talk about the statue of the horseman. It was, he said, quite interesting for a civic work; certainly the sculptor had been able to communicate a certain dignity and courage. I nodded. It seemed that Max was artificially drawing out the conversation, as if he wanted to strengthen our acquaintance. I took a step further away. 'Of course,' he said, 'you have already seen the church?'

Before I could say that we had Jean replied, truthfully, that we had not.

'You should not miss it, because it is very famous. Mrs Tinnion, would you like us to take you there? It is only a short way, and the interior is very beautiful. But also, I think, quite bizarre.' I could tell that he was pleased by his use of the last word.

'That would be nice,' Jean agreed, ignoring the sly cautionary nudge I gave her.

The church was cream-coloured, with a bulbous, Eastern-

8

looking tower and narrow leaded windows. An old man dozed by the main door. A dog lay on the ground beside him, one ear flat, the other cocked. Max put some coins on a plate by the man's feet and then pushed at the iron-studded door.

'Is he an official?' Jean whispered as we passed.

Max answered, 'He will raise a warning if anyone suspicious approaches. He is tolerated, that's all.'

Within the church the air was cooler. I could smell cold stone and wax. The interior was dark wood, flagstones, pale columns, speckled marble, gilded angels. The windows brightened and dimmed as clouds passed, their colours fading then swelling – gold, azure, blood. The central aisle led through rows of ornately carved pews to a double altar of helical columns as dark as ebony, but twined around with silvered leaves and gilded vines. At the base of the altar, behind a Byzantine crucifix of solid gold, there was a large glass case.

As we approached I realised that the case contained two mummified bodies dressed in jewelled robes and reclining on satin. Jean faltered, then walked forward. I could feel her shiver. Bruno walked quickly ahead of us, and stared into the dead faces as if into a great mystery.

'They come many kilometres to see this,' Max said, speaking in German now. 'It is a bishop and a nun – look, you can see by the clothes they wear. I have tried to photograph them, but I cannot get permission.' He nodded to the far side of the church. Two men in black vestments stood watching us.

'They're horrible,' Jean said, staring through the glass.

Nearness revealed more detail. The desiccated, vacant faces showed nothing, but a camouflaging vitality shone from the precious stones that had been set in the eye sockets, and the ash-coloured mouths gaped to show jewels set among the blackened teeth.

'Horrible?' Max asked. 'Yes, perhaps. But look at the richness of the garments – that is gold thread; think of the weeks, the months that must have gone into such embroidery. That, I think, is silk. And those are real pearls around the woman's neck.'

I noticed that the bishop's visible fingers had elaborate rings placed on them, although beneath them the knuckles were as yellow as the bones of a dead sheep. On the nun, however, there was only a bride-of-Christ ring, a thick band around a shrunken finger. For some reason I found this especially disconcerting, but I could not show my emotion with Max standing so close to me.

'I am told that they died terrible deaths,' he said, 'although no doubt they died for what they believed in. What would lead them to such an end? Bad luck, fate? They may even have had a chance to turn their backs on destiny, and live out their lives without pain, but without glory as well. Look at them – they have become a shrine, a symbol.'

'A symbol for what?' I asked.

'For the nature of suffering, of course. It is said that if a sick person touches these fingers then he will be miraculously cured. That is why the cases are locked, and that is why we are being watched.'

'I feel quite ill,' Jean said.

'Of course,' Max continued, lowering his voice, 'what happened to these people must have been an insane and foolish tragedy. These priests know how to turn such a disaster into a justification and a triumph – one that has lasted for hundreds of years, and will last for much longer.' He smiled confidentially at me. 'Do you not admire people like that?' he asked. 'They are men after my own heart. I, too, must learn to make a myth from the weak and the failed.'

I smiled wanly, determined not to ask him to explain himself.

He chuckled as if he found my reaction amusing, and clapped Bruno on the shoulder. 'Come,' he said, 'we must return.'

We walked back down the aisle, but when I was a few yards from the altar I turned to look back at the macabre exhibits. A powerful beam of sunlight struck through a high window and made the finery glow and sparkle, so that the bodies were lost within a glittering cocoon of reflection.

Max insisted on taking us back to the Seematter's in his car. On the way he chatted, apparently inconsequentially, of the places they had visited over the last few days, and of the natural history specimens Bruno had collected. Jean talked to the boy in simple, halting German. He rewarded her persistence with a few perfunctory remarks.

That evening, after we had eaten, Max joined us while we sat at the front of the pension with our backs to the mural. Picturesque from a distance, the mural could be seen to be crudely executed if examined more closely. Two hunters struck melodramatically heroic poses while a fleeing chamois leaped an impossible chasm on legs that were anatomically unsound. Otto had already talked of having it repainted. A man further down the valley could do it, he told me; a man renowned for his draughtsman's talent and his painter's eye. Or perhaps, he mused, if the man were cheap enough, he could have an entirely new painting done, of a new subject – something heroic, but something unusual.

Jean was smoking a cigarette. She had already decided to give up smoking, for (she claimed) we could no longer afford such luxuries. Once or twice, however, she indulged herself.

Max sat beside us. Bruno had gone to bed because he was tired, but Max sat close to us as if he had a right to be there. All the time he had the demeanour of a man who was giving information on the understanding that he would receive some in return.

Our talk was steered by him so that it became too personal much too quickly.

Jean told him that we had been married less than a month. 'Really?' he asked, one doubtful eyebrow raised, before he congratulated us. In the church he had talked as if he had some grasp of the values of gold and precious stones; perhaps he was wondering why her wedding-ring was so plain and inexpensive.

I looked at him and did not give anything away by my expression.

'This is a wonderful part of the world to come to,' he said. 'And these are beautiful mountains. I had hoped to climb some myself, but Bruno is more interested in life in the valleys. But perhaps you will be exploring them, Mr Tinnion? You look like an active man.'

To scale down a truth seemed less hazardous than telling a detectable lie. I told him a friend would join us soon, and that we may do a little climbing together.

'You are on honeymoon, and yet you are meeting a friend? Surely your wife must be forgiving as well as charming.'

'That's why I married her,' I said.

I was annoyed, but Jean did not appear to be. Instead she countered by asking Max his own reasons for being at the Seematters'.

Max pursued his lips, considered a moment, and then told us his story.

He and his mother were now Bruno's guardians. It was not easy. The boy had begun to lose himself in his interests, but that was only to be expected. He had passed through a bad time recently. But Max was a single man who had to travel a lot for his work, and he was worried about his mother's health. A boy as young as Bruno was difficult for an older lady to look after. A fortnight's holiday here was a perfect break in routine. While they were away, his mother was visiting her sister in Frankfurt.

'We live in Munich,' he went on. 'It is a fine place. I travel throughout Germany, and further, but I always love to come home. Now I take Bruno boating on the Isar, or show him our museums and those hidden corners of the city which only a few people know. He, too, loves the city. He was a little disappointed when the ornamental gardens of the Königsplatz were replaced by granite slabs, but soon he will grow to like the new architecture.'

'He's settled with you?' Jean asked.

'I believe so. I had to be in Berlin recently – I was at the Olympics, in fact – and during that time he cried a lot. But he is happier now.'

'Are the boy's parents dead?' she asked.

I winced at her directness, but he did not take offence.

'It is a sad story, Mrs Tinnion. The boy's mother was no good. She deserted the child. His father – my only brother – was killed in an accident at his work a short time later. We had to change our lives for the sake of Bruno. I had to buy a bigger house, and move him and my mother into it with me. But I do not regret it.'

'And *his* mother?'

'Vanished. To another man, I suppose. My brother was a good husband and father, and yet she deserted him. I have no desire to see her again. And she has given up any rights she may have had over Bruno.'

'She must have had her reasons, Herr Volkwein.'

She seemed to me to be at the dangerous edge of things, but Max merely said, 'No doubt.' When he looked at her, I could see a certain craftiness in his eyes.

I stared past him and looked down the valley. I was hoping to hear a motorcycle approaching, or perhaps see its light as it curved round one of the distant bends, but there was no sign.

Shortly afterwards Max stood up to take his leave. Once again he insisted on shaking hands, and this time he held mine in his for several seconds while he looked closely at me.

'It is an unusual name,' he said; 'tell me – should I know you?'

I shook my head. 'Not so unusual, not in England. And no, I don't think you should.'

'I have not read your name anywhere?'

'I doubt it.'

'My memory,' he said, and tapped the side of his head while he smiled, 'it must be playing tricks.' Then he clicked his heels as best he could, and bade us goodnight.

I waited until he was out of earshot before I spoke to Jean.

'I don't like him,' I said. 'He makes me uneasy.'

'Really? I think he's quite interesting. And think of what he's done for that boy. I admire people like that.'

'There's a certain cold smugness about him, don't you think? And I would take a bet that his politics are far from liberal.'

'What does it matter what his politics are? It's what he's done that matters.'

I stood up. 'Maybe you're right,' I said.

I walked down the road for a few yards. Small insects swarmed in the darkness, and above my head the night was full of stars.

When I returned Jean put her hand in the hair at the back of my head. 'My poor darling,' she said, 'is your friend so important to you?' She took my earlobe between her teeth and exerted a slight pressure.

'I thought he might be here by now. That's all.'

'Shall I tell you something? I don't care if he doesn't come. I'm happy as we are now, just the two of us, together at last.'

'But he's the reason we're here,' I said. Until I saw her face I did not think I was being unkind.

When we went to our room she lay on the bed while I stood on the balcony, gazing into the massive darkness and listening to the tiny noises that murmured against the silence. After a while she tiptoed out to join me, took me by the hand, and led me back into the bedroom.

During the night I woke with the certainty that Hansi had arrived. Cool air spilled into the room through the french windows. Jean's body lay facing mine, the nightdress risen around her waist so that the curve of her hip was made ivory by moonlight. I left the bed and walked to the balustrade, feeling the grain of the wood beneath my feet. Beneath the stars, below the blackness of the mountains, the fields were a flimsy grey. On top of the nearest rise I could see an indistinct pale smudge which could be a tent. I watched for only a short while, then got back into bed. Jean stirred and, in sleep, put her arm across me. I was comfortable and warm, and fell asleep almost immediately.

At sunrise I woke up again, and saw that I had been right – a tent was pitched on the rise, near to a solitary chestnut tree.

Even though it was early, the morning was already warm. I left Jean sleeping and let myself out of the Seematters' front door. There were noises from the kitchen as I passed.

I crossed the deserted road and walked up a grassy incline drenched with dew. In the angled light the silk of spiders could be seen trailing in thousands of brilliant strands across the hill. Small beetles rose from my steps, their wings shining, and the grass rasped across my boots like a cow's tongue across a hand.

The tent was small and drab, the colour of camouflage. Across the valley, its face in full sunlight, the Versücherin was colossal, sharp, and chilling. Leading up to the tent was a thin track of flattened grass which was slowly springing back into position, stalk by stalk, and around the guy-ropes the ground had been trampled. A motorcycle stood near the tree, its casings gleaming but its tyres coated with broken stems and dried mud. High up in the air larks were singing, and from far away I could hear cowbells.

The tent flap was open, and fastened back. Inside Hansi lay asleep, naked but for a pair of loose shorts. At rest his face was untroubled, almost angelic. His breath was light, his ribcage moved only slightly, and under the lids his eyes darted, as if he dreamed.

I crouched, entered the cramped confines of the tent, and spoke his name. He awoke immediately. 'Ernst,' he said sleepily. He called me Ernst or Ernest as the occasion demanded. I extended a hand, but he sat up and embraced me, and suddenly we began to giggle like schoolboys at the pleasure, and faint absurdity, of our meeting.

'I thought I would surprise you,' I said.

'You have done; it is *good* to see you.' He struggled to his knees

15

and put his hand on my shoulder. I could feel the strength in it, even though the grip was light. 'Forgive me, there is something I must do.'

We crawled awkwardly from the tent. Hansi faced the tree and urinated on the grass, only partly turned away from me. I looked in the other direction.

'I arrived about two,' he said over his shoulder, 'so I camped here. I was coming to meet you after breakfast.'

'Eat with me. The Seematters are expecting you.'

Hansi came back and leaned on the saddle. 'You said *me*. Does that mean that you are on your own?'

'No. She's asleep.' I tugged a blade of grass from near my feet. 'What I said in the letter was true.'

He nodded, then indicated the motorcycle like a ringmaster displaying an amazing act. 'You like this? It's a *feast* of a machine.' For some time he described the motorcycle's qualities and style as if it was a thoroughbred horse. 'I cut quite a dash riding it, Ernst. Some people are even jealous of me.'

'Hansi, before we go, you and I must understand each other.'

He turned away to reach into the tent for his clothes. 'We have always tried to do that.'

'Yes. But you must understand about Jean.'

He had not unbuttoned his shirt, and now he pulled it down over his head like a sweater. 'Your letter left some things which were not explained,' he said, looking out of the collar with his hair tousled. 'But you and I have always been the best of friends. We don't have to clear the air.'

'We're registered as Mr and Mrs Tinnion.'

He nodded, rolling up his shirtsleeves.

'We're not married.'

'No?'

'No.'

'I thought not. Your letter was unclear.'

'I'm sorry. It was either tell you the minimum or write

16

page after page. I thought it would be better to wait until we met.'

Hansi pulled on his trousers and buttoned them. 'What shall I call her?'

'Jean.'

'And who knows she is not your wife?'

'Just you.'

He was pulling on his boots. 'I am honoured, then.'

'Her real name is Mrs Jean Swarbrick.'

'So there is a Mr Swarbrick?'

'Left behind. In England.'

Hansi laced his boots, then clapped his hands together. 'Come, we shall ride down the hill.'

'One more thing.'

He looked at me in mock surprise. 'Something else? I did not know you were a man with so many secrets.'

'She knows about the climb, but no one else does. I had to tell her. But I don't think she realises how dangerous it is. We don't talk about it much. I don't even know if she thinks about it all that often.'

'Of course,' he said guardedly, as if he expected me to express doubts about the wisdom of the climb.

'I'm trying to say that she doesn't know anything about our sport, Hansi. Before she met me, a mountain was just an area of darkness on a map, topped with white if it was high enough. As the time approaches, I don't know how she will react.'

'You've told her as much as you can?'

'Yes. She thinks it's a big adventure, a game.' I dropped the grass stalk when I saw that I had mangled it. 'She'll have to face up to reality now.'

'There can be very little delay, Ernst. Your arrangement with the lady is your concern, but it must not be allowed to delay us or affect our confidence. We must be single-minded – you know that to be true. The weather cannot be controlled, but it could not be better than it is at the moment. I am as fit as I can be, and our equipment is the best. Have you any other doubts?'

I shook my head.

'We have *very* little time,' he went on. 'The summer will be over soon, and next year there are other groups who will be on the Versücherin. There could even be some here soon, within the next few days. We must do it quickly if we are to do it at all.'

'I agree.'

'Be honest with me – why are you here?'

'For the wall, Hansi. I shouldn't have to tell you that.'

He smiled, put a fist to my shoulder, and climbed on the motorcycle. 'Hold on to me,' he said.

We began to ride down the hill. The grass hissed and parted under the wheels and I could feel the swell and dip of earth pass upwards through the frame. Hansi veered from side to side, riding the gradient like a huge wave, and the smell of clover blew in our faces. At the bottom of the incline, in a daredevil mood, Hansi took the machine into a tight curve so that the rear wheel juddered and grit scattered from beneath it. I tensed myself, half expecting to topple, and hung on to him more tightly than on any climb. He chuckled like a boy pleased with his own simple joke, and we came to rest.

Hansi wheeled the cycle to a standstill, then parked it beneath a trail of honeysuckle which hung from a trellis near the door. 'They'll be delighted to see you again,' I said. I had already looked in Otto's scrapbook. One of the most recent cuttings had been a description of the last days of the Hinterstoisser-Kurz climb. Hansi's name was mentioned among the rescue team.

I led the way inside.

The Seematters fussed over Hansi. Otto still went out on to the mountains, and although his range was decreasing year by year he was still capable of climbing the east ridge of the Versücherin without difficulty. He was always eager to tell climbing anecdotes, but always pretended that he did not wish to, so that he had to be persuaded. Sometimes he would make half-joking references to climbers such as us, and call us ladder-makers, rock-scramblers. Neither Hansi, me, nor anyone else had ever taken offence. Indeed, Otto had often sat with us and pointed out important climbs in his scrapbook, apparently as proud of the new generation as he was of his own. Now he and Clara asked Hansi about his job, his health, his recent climbs. Otto shook his head over the death of Toni Kurz – such a promising young man, and killed so tragically early in his career. Clara asked if, one day soon, Hansi would bring a beautiful young wife to stay with them, just as I had done. Hansi demurred – marriage was not for him, he said, not just yet.

At last, understanding that we wished to talk alone, Clara led Otto into the kitchen. By this time the other Swiss guests had arrived, and sat waiting for their breakfast.

'Keep your voice down,' Hansi murmured, lowering his own like a conspirator in a spy thriller.

'They're nothing to worry about,' I said. Now that we had sat down, Hansi had placed his hands on the table-top. For the first time I noticed that the ends of his fingers were white, as if the circulation in them had become poor.

'We mustn't let word get back to our competitors,' he said.

'Hansi, no one could get there before us. Not now. There are no other *serious* parties in the valley.'

'A large team, fully equipped, could move much more quickly than we could. What would happen if such a team arrived now?'

'It won't happen.'

'Besides,' he went on, 'some people are fools, and would step on to the north wall even if it meant wrecking our chances. Until the first icefield the face is not difficult. And I have had my fill of being in rescue parties.' He leaned closer to me. 'I worked it all out when I was here in the spring. No one knew I was here, but I camped in the fields, surveyed the face from every angle, watched it at all times of day to study perspectives. No one knows more about that mountain than I do – no one. But I have not even set foot on the wall. It must be done properly, honourably, and in accordance with what everyone expects.'

At the other end of the room the Swiss had begun to talk animatedly. One spoke so loudly that he nearly drowned out Hansi.

'We must go up by the east ridge and place some stores within the summit cairn, just in case we have to spend an extra night on the face. The true attempt will have to start around midnight. There is an abandoned building near the foot of the mountain which can be used as a base. In spring it was barred, but the door was broken. I have already spent one night there. Our equipment must be trimmed to the essentials. We take enough for two nights, maybe three, that's all. We do not need any superfluous weight.'

'And we set off when?'

'A couple of days. We dare not wait any longer.'

'And the route?'

He touched his temple with his finger. 'There is only one possible route, Ernst. I know mountains so well now that they will give up their secrets if I ask them. Some may see nothing but precipices, a wilderness of ice heaped on top of rock, but I can see a route. Just like a general can see victory in an empty field on the day before battle, I can see a way up. I already know where we will struggle, and where we will rest. We have nothing to fear.'

'Except the weather.'

'Perhaps.'

'And our nerves?'

He laughed. 'Never.'

As Clara served us breakfast Max and Bruno came into the room. They sat in the far corner. Bruno had a butterfly net, which he leaned against a wall. Max nodded at me, and regarded Hansi with a cool interest. Sensitive to their arrival, and to the lessening of noise as the guests began to eat, Hansi began to talk about teaching. As he ate breakfast he began to act out the role of someone who had escaped his normal job for the sake of a few days' light activity. Hansi was a sports master, and was enthusiastic about one of his pupils who was a gifted runner. For some time he recited a catalogue of the boy's achievements and speculated on his future. I, in turn, told him how I had continued to visit the Lake District, and that I had recently sought out some locations described by Wordsworth. Hansi knew almost nothing about literature, so I could talk for several minutes on this. We were still relaxed, and drinking more coffee, when the Volkweins got to their feet. Bruno bustled past, eyes down, the net held in front of him like a flag, but Max stopped by our table. With my eyes I tried to signal to Hansi that I knew nothing of this.

'You are too modest, Mr Tinnion,' Max said; 'you did not tell me who your friend would be.' He clicked his heels and inclined the upper half of his body toward Hansi. 'Forgive me, but you are Herr Kirchner, I think.'

Hansi rose and shook Max's hand, the chair-leg grating on the floor. He wore an expression of sheepish pride at being recognised.

'I knew I was right,' Max said, smirking, 'and it is an honour to meet you, sir. My name is Max Volkwein – I do not know if you have heard of me.' His voice rose slightly, giving his words the air of a question. Hansi glanced at me and I responded with a tiny shrug; I had no idea why Max should think he could be known. 'Ah,' he said, making it sound that Hansi was somehow disadvantaged because he did not recognise Max. 'No matter,' he continued; 'I am a photographer, and, if I may say so without sounding vain, some of my work is very well known. I must let you see some examples, if you have time.'

Hansi sank back down on to his chair. He appeared perplexed and did not respond to the suggestion.

'So,' Max said, 'you two gentlemen will be climbing around here?' He must have noticed Hansi's eyes flick towards the Swiss, for he immediately corrected himself. 'But of course,' he said contritely, as if he had been guilty of an unthinking breach of etiquette, 'I understand perfectly.'

Hansi made a motion with his hand like that of a generous pontiff giving absolution, but there was no brotherhood in his face. Max then explained that he and Bruno were to explore further up the valley where, he hoped, they would be able to trap a particular kind of butterfly which had wings of cobalt blue.

After he had gone, Hansi sat quietly for a few moments.

'What's up?' I asked.

'He knows.'

'Don't be absurd. I haven't said a thing, and neither has Jean. He's just curious, that's all, and too inquisitive for his own good.'

'He recognised me.'

'You're in Otto's scrapbook, that's why.'

'Perhaps. But he knows why we're here, Ernst. We must decide what to do about it.'

The Swiss rose to their feet and began to walk outside, still chattering loudly. At the same time I saw Jean enter the room. The Swiss stopped by us, looking upwards at the photographs of the young Seematters and commenting on them. Jean edged her way past them and stood at our table.

I stood up. 'Hansi,' I said, 'may I present my wife.'

2

FOR A LONG TIME WE DID NOT SPEAK, BUT WALKED THROUGH A COOL silence where the only sounds were those of the clinking of metal pegs and, from far away but distinct, the hiss of falling water. We could have been the only living things at the very centre of the world.

Hansi kept glancing up at the stars, estimating the arrival of dawn from their position in the sky. We crossed the rolling grassy hillocks with ease. At this hour they were the colour of ash, and Hansi had to direct the lantern light when we came to dark pools of shadow beside the rocks. By the time we neared the debris at the foot of the wall, the eastern sky had begun to lighten with a dim, satiny texture, but above us the huge bulk of the north face was a cold and featureless black. Suddenly, full-throated and repetitive, a bird began to sing.

To begin with we had been able to walk with a regular, unforced motion. Now, picking our way among strewn boulders and unreliable fragments of stone, we had to step as carefully as if we were on the wall itself. Hansi held the lantern to illuminate our path, and I followed his light. Our boots scraped and clicked on the bare rock.

Now that we were so close I was filled with apprehension and foreboding, and it seemed to me that we were fools, drunk with the egotism of the adventurous, risking our lives for nothing more than fame, about to sacrifice ourselves for the sake of an ideal.

Perhaps, without meaning to, I lagged behind. Hansi sensed my hesitation and stopped, his legs braced on a fractured boulder, and he held the lantern so that he could see my face more clearly. I shielded my eyes and looked up at him. His felt hat was tilted at an easygoing, almost rakish angle, and his eyes were direct and honest. The closeness of the lantern made his lips appear full, almost feminine. I thought of Jean, alone in her bed at the Seematters'. 'Ernest,' he said cheerfully, 'it is too soon to be so far behind.'

Standing in the way that he did, and hung about with rope and pegs, the axe glinting in its leather sling, he looked both invincible and reassuring. Not for the first time, I was comforted and given direction by him.

He lowered the light, and his face broke in a smile. 'You know what Max would say – so long as we have the will, all things are possible.' He pointed to the east. 'And look over there.'

The far range of mountains had their summit ridges edged with a brilliant sharpness, and within the greyness of the valley I could see distance and depth begin to return.

'Already the top of this mountain is in sunlight,' Hansi continued, 'so why are we wasting time? Let's go to meet it!'

Walking in unison we threaded our way across the rubble-strewn well of the face. The landscape was lunar, a wilderness of shards and grit which crunched beneath us. Each surface was dusted with a cold gravel that could be swept away with the side of a hand. As soon as the sun warmed the slopes, fragments of rock would shower towards us. Despite my new confidence, I still found it easy to imagine us beaten back very quickly by a constant hail of tiny stones.

Soon the ground steepened so that it was possible to move upwards side by side at a rhythmic, unthinking pace. I climbed automatically, grasping rock, turf, and coarse heather. After a while I heard dogs barking far below. They were noises from a world I was leaving, and they reminded me of the distance I had put between myself and Jean. Across to our left the sun lifted above the rim of mountains, and its light moved across the valley in a great declining plane. As dawn crept towards us down the wall, I could see the peaks, the flanks of mountains, the wooded slopes and finally the fields of the valley floor given colour, perspective, detail. Everything became endlessly, stunningly clear. The sound of goatbells drifted upwards from a broad swath of pasture, and church bells chimed from a faraway spire.

Here we came across stars and radiants of deliquescent ice, as if a huge shield had fallen the day before and shattered as it tumbled. Hansi picked up a handful. The large watery grains dribbled through his fingers.

'It will have vanished in an hour or so,' he pronounced, and turned a piece over with his boot. I could see thin layers fused into each other. 'From one of the high cornices,' he said.

'You think it came away by itself?'

'It must have.'

'You don't think someone else made this break away? Someone who might have got ahead of us?'

He shook his head. 'It fell of its own accord, I think. This isn't good news, Ernst. The temperature on the face may be *too* high. But let us hope, yes?'

We looked up, and could not see the upper reaches of the wall. From now onwards our view could only be partial, restricted, and misleading.

If we had not known that a hot sun had warmed the face, we would soon have found out, for an hour later we were in sunshine that made us sweat. Away to our left thin splinters of rock began to fall from where they had been loosened. They fell gracefully down the lower slopes, striking the inclines and bouncing outward, and making a noise like a muffled, spasmodic rattle. Beneath us the shadows in the fields had shortened and dissolved, but because of our position on the face our own shadows were flung over to our right and made elongated and angular.

There was little to disturb us, other than when Hansi scared a raven which exploded from a narrow flattened area and soared around us, crying hoarsely.

We made Friendly Ledge by early afternoon, and hauled ourselves on to it. We crouched for a while until our breathing steadied. We agreed that the temperature was higher than we had expected, and both of us were pleased with the easiness of the climb so far.

At its broadest part Friendly Ledge was the width of two men, and no more than twelve feet long. It was covered in broken rock, water ice, and green slippery algae. We had expected it to be more hospitable.

After ten minutes Hansi stood on tiptoe, his boots lodged on the lip of our shelter, and peered upwards. I followed his gaze. Tall backbones of rock reared up and away from us. Where the sun struck the wall the surface was livid and fierce, where the wall was angled away from the sun it was gloomy and severe. Quite suddenly Hansi drew back his hand and extended it towards me. Centrally placed in the palm of his glove was a small fragment of rock. 'It came rolling down,' he said in a matter-of-fact manner.

Small as the piece was, I realised that there was a danger of slippage directly above us. 'Hear anything?' I asked, but he shook his head.

I wondered how many people were watching us at that very minute. I could imagine that there would be hundreds of them already, and that the higher we went, the more our spectators would number. Eventually, as we neared the summit, there would be thousands lining the roads, sitting on balconies, standing in fields, their binoculars and telescopes all trained on us. I had a thrill of juvenile pleasure at the thought.

We waited until the sun crawled across the higher surfaces then vanished out of sight. It was mid-afternoon. As soon as the sun had vanished, the face began to cool.

While we waited we ate an apple each. 'We could have made it,' I said.

'Possibly.'

But I was wrong. Shortly afterwards a trickle of tiny stones began to fall towards us, some cartwheeling outwards with a thin reedy noise, others clattering purposefully on the rock. One or two even landed on our ledge. Along with them came a mist of icy rain, like droplets blown from an unseen waterfall.

We tensed, waiting to see if the avalanche would cease or worsen.

In less than a minute we had our answer. Large stones tumbled furiously around us, striking sparks from the limestone where they crashed into it. We crouched in defensive postures, trying to make our bodies as small as possible and hoisting the rucksacks onto our backs as shields. The stones whirred past or cracked sharply as they hit, and smaller pieces pattered the rucksack canvas like hail. I was hit on the knuckles, and yelped. I withdrew my hand, tugged off the glove, and expected to see a wound that would drive us back down the Versücherin, but only a small piece of skin had been knocked away. Hansi lifted himself fractionally, saw that I had not been badly hurt, and buried himself again beneath his rucksack.

Eventually the bombardment thinned, then stopped, the sound dying away like the passing of a battle. We became conscious of our own discomfort, for we were bent, on our knees, and with cold water seeping into our clothes. We peered out as if from a burrow, but everything had cleared and there was no indication of any further falls.

Before we roped up we urinated on the rock, and fastidiously avoided having the streams run onto our boots. I wondered if observers could see what we were doing.

Hansi nodded at the rock that faced us. 'Me?' I asked.

'Do you want to?'

And of course I was pleased that he was allowing me to be front man, and considered it an honour to lead the way up a series of sodden, gritty verticals. I was conscious, too, that in allowing me to do this he was keeping the more dangerous and challenging parts for himself.

We moved across to the right so that we would be away from any further falls, and I ascended the face with such concentration that, after a while, I had the odd, unreal sensation that all of my world was reducible to a few square feet of cliff just in front of me. I was concerned only with grip, balance, leverage; the rest of my existence, and all other emotion, became peripheral to the necessities of the climb. My beliefs, my future, my affair had the characteristics of something imagined, and therefore changeable.

A noise like a distant hailshower drifted across the face, and we stopped, although we could not tell where it had come from. I looked down. Hansi was fastened to the rock at the end of a slack rope. Beneath him the wall plummeted, then swept into fields, treetops, streams, all as if seen by a bird. He nodded his head to indicate that I should go on, and pulled in some of the slack.

'The vertical crack?' I asked, my voice travelling easily through the clear air. He nodded.

I set off again, but half an hour later he tugged at the rope as I was resting, and when I looked down at him he pointed urgently at the rock we were fastened on. I peered intently at its grain, wondering if I had missed a vital clue to the solution of the ascent. Soon I noticed that in several places it had been chipped as if by the blow of a hammer. Astonished, I looked back at Hansi.

'It's all across here,' he called.

'Men? Or a rock fall?'

'Definitely not men. We must have wandered back into the path of a chute.'

Nothing moved, apart from the raven which soared past us then lifted against a sky of brilliant blue.

I licked my lips. 'Are we in danger?'

'Saved by the temperature, perhaps. There could be nothing left to fall.'

We agreed that I should anchor myself while Hansi investigated the surface to either side of us. The raven casually rode the updraughts of air, its harsh sonorous call echoing around the cliffs.

Eventually we moved further to the right, where Hansi could find no strike marks, and he took the lead. I found it pleasant to be at the lower end of the rope again; I had few decisions to make, and I became relaxed and confident. Quite suddenly, with the clarity of a vision, I believed that the Versücherin would be ours.

Jean pursued knowledge. She expected me to have a grounding in subjects about which I knew little, and I would find myself persuaded to talk about European history, the development of art, or the primary beliefs of religion. Much of what I said was speculative, but disguised by confidence. All the time Jean's questions, and her digressions, suggested an insatiable but undisciplined desire to learn. Often I wondered if, when I had been emptied of everything I had to say, I would have to sustain her interest by fabrication alone.

Before she met me Jean had already cultivated, and discarded, several enthusiasms. She came to me because she had decided that English poetry, particularly Romantic poetry, would provide her with insight and, perhaps, contentment.

I took an evening class once a week. It helped augment my teacher's salary; it also provided me with an opportunity to discuss literature, or at least discourse on it. If ever I returned to Switzerland I would be able to say that I had taught the classics of my native land.

It helped, too, in salving my periodically active social conscience. I believed that working people had the right to learn about culture, literature, ideas. I believed that they were eager for knowledge and that, given time, Britain could become a truly socialist country. At times I found my beliefs to be in conflict with my own wishes and needs, as I found that my ideal political state was very far removed from the country I had grown up in, and to which I often returned.

In fact most of my students were lower middle class, usually women, and surprisingly reluctant to express an opinion or even read a chosen passage. They were embarrassed, and sat hunched over their texts like vagrants over hostel soup. It took a while before I realised that, in some way, they felt intimidated by me. I suspected, too, that they thought that poetry should be read in an unreal, fluting voice, and that it should possess, not immediacy, but a kind of simple-minded nebulousness. I broadened my accent to make myself more approachable, but also to coarsen the sound of the poetry. They were not persuaded by this.

Before she enrolled for my Romanticism course Jean had begun to learn Italian, and become bored; studied theosophy, and found that she could not believe it, and listened to classical music, which she could not enjoy. Each of these pursuits had held the promise of newness, elevation, insight. She had been disappointed each time.

She arrived with a friend. It was evident that neither of them had the financial uncertainties which worried so many of my students. The friend wore different clothes for each meeting, and ostentatiously offered cigarettes from a lady's silver case. As if seeking to demonstrate her membership of the select, she often mentioned the names of local dignitaries, but she had nothing to say about poetry. After a few weeks she stopped coming, leaving Jean to attend on her own. I did not see her friend again until, shortly before we left, I dined at the Swarbricks'.

At first Jean was reserved, although her desire to learn was almost palpable. She watched me all the time, seeming to hang on every word.

Harry had agreed that she should take the course. He had

humoured her other interests, too. 'Whims', he called them. For he recognised that, after only a few years of marriage, his wife had become moody and unsettled. For a while, perhaps, he had thought that a child would provide the answer, but since one had failed to come along he let Jean occupy her time in harmless pursuits. Even so, whenever she talked about them, Harry was critical. He had supposed that Italian was of some use, albeit an impractical one because he had no intention of ever going to Italy. German would have been better, for the German market was expanding and, he believed, they were the kind of people who would refuse to talk English out of spite. Theosophy, music and literature were, however, immature and womanly. They had little to do with the real world, which was an elaborate but tangible construction of business, politics, law, economics.

He also expressed a special distaste for my course. There were, he knew, certain poets who had been far from reputable characters. When Jean pressed him, he elaborated with unspecific hints of effeminacy, debauchery and political extremism. When Jean told me his opinions I found their naïvety both amusing and depressing. But if Harry had not been convinced of the essential powerlessness of literature, and its intrinsic uselessness, he may well have forbidden her to attend. As it was, Harry saw in her reading an equivalent to the singing of a popular song – something ephemeral, mildly emotional, but most of all unimportant.

Jean had to be coaxed before she would talk. Later, she confessed that she was nervous about saying anything in front of me, as she was afraid that I would heartlessly dissect it. She felt provincial, educationally impoverished, unable to put her feelings into words.

I told her I did not make such judgements, and she became annoyed at my flippancy. What could I know of her kind of life, she demanded; from my position of experience and privilege, surely I would find it impossible not to judge her?

And yet I felt she was the one who possessed privilege and

ease. Even though she had not been educated to my standards, she was far wealthier than I was, or was ever likely to be. I admired her, and was even occasionally jealous of her.

She read less deeply than I, and with little critical consideration, but she read more sympathetically, and often more passionately. Nor did she confine herself to the boundaries of the course. When I digressed to talk about German Romanticism she asked for more detail, and the next week arrived with a copy of *Faust*. She was, she claimed, inspired by it.

If a work affected her, she would proclaim its virtues with a zeal that was powerful if uninformed. I tried to inculcate coolness, objectivity, perspective; she wanted force, passion, and most of all transcendence. It soon became obvious that literature was feeding a need that was deep within her, and yet I saw little sign of any lasting satisfaction or contentment. Instead her reading made her increasingly aware of an intensity, real or imagined, which her own life lacked.

I wondered, then, if I should discourage her. I did not.

Instead I told her that I had some Goethe in the original German, which she could borrow if she wished.

'I don't speak German,' she said; 'I'd like to, but I don't.'

'That's a pity. I could teach you, if you wished.'

'You would? That would be wonderful.'

I cleared my throat. 'Of course, I'd have to charge you. But it wouldn't be much.'

Harry paid for this as well.

I wondered about my own motives, and tried to believe that they were merely financial. At most I thought that Jean and I may have a mild flirtation, nothing more.

It was the beginning of winter. Sleety rain could be seen in the gaslights. I waited nervously in my lodgings. She was five minutes late, and for a while I thought that she may have decided not to come after all.

She wore a fur coat with a collar that was cold and sparkled

32

with formless snow. The fur smelled faintly of mothballs. She shivered, clasped her hands, and sat down in a high-backed chair. She looked lost, out of her depth, but determined. I had put more coal on the fire, but warmth did not reach to where she sat even though I could see flame reflected in her eyes.

I was fluent but offhand, as if my knowledge of German was boundless and refined. I wondered if she sensed my desperation. I had become sharply aware of the dinginess of my rooms. Even though I had dusted the shelves and moved a chair so that it blocked her view of a damp patch on the wallpaper, my surroundings were evidently drab and unpleasant. I felt like apologising for them, for my bachelor's untidiness and muddle. Used to larger spaces, cleanliness and comfort, she looked prim within surroundings such as mine.

'I didn't expect to find you living like this,' she said after a while. 'I thought your circumstances would be more grand.'

'These are hard times,' I said.

She looked round the room.

'Mrs Swarbrick, my income is nothing like as large as you may think. I need to do private tuition, otherwise I couldn't even afford this. As you can see, I live frugally. I spend money on books and travel. Those are my essentials.'

Thinking I was demanding payment already, she opened her purse.

'Please,' I said, 'there's no need to pay until the lesson is over.'

She adjusted her hands on her lap. 'You go back to Switzerland when you can?'

'Yes.'

'And you climb there.'

'I didn't think I'd mentioned it.'

'When you were talking about the influence of landscape on poetry . . .'

I nodded. 'Of course.'

'And when you were talking about Coleridge, you mentioned

his climb in the Lake District. You said his description was infused with ideas of grandeur and freedom.'

'He certainly conveys some of the excitement of climbing, Mrs Swarbrick. Coleridge writes with a kind of controlled delirium about his climb. Everyone knows what that sensation is.'

'You learned climbing when you were a boy?'

'I spent much of my boyhood near my father's timber mill. It was in a Swiss valley – the mill's closed now, I'm afraid. But, when you know German a little, you will be able to tell that I have a Swiss accent. That comes from my childhood. And there was a rock near to where we lived. It looked like a buttress against a hill, because it had been scoured by glacier ice, then eroded.'

'I've never seen a glacier,' she said; 'perhaps one day I shall.'

At first the climb had been a mere escapade, and I had thought myself daring and adventurous merely to get a few feet up the side. Later, when the thrill of the misdeed had passed, I had begun to explore the crag systematically, but with neither rope nor correct footwear. Once or twice I had found myself apparently cragfast, trapped on the face without any means of escape. Always I had managed to control my nerves, and always I had found a way. My confidence was such that I became euphoric. I sought to maroon myself on the rock, to manoeuvre my body into a position where, balanced on my toes and with my fingers in the narrowest of ledges, I could not see where to go next. At such moments I would experience both elation and calm. I knew that if I let it the fear of falling would tug at me like something dark and unmanning, and inhabit me with panic. I kept fear at bay by a princely confidence in my own abilities and destiny. In an extraordinary, unquestionable way, I was in harmony with both the rock and myself.

'When I had exhausted the crag,' I continued, 'I moved on to harder climbs. By then I had bought a pair of *tricouni* boots – those have a special arrangement of nails in the sole.'

34

'It all sounds very exciting, Mr Tinnion. I'm sure that you make an excellent climber.'

I shrugged modestly. I did not think she would be able to understand exactly how good I was.

'That's where I first met my friend Hansi,' I said; 'he and I have climbed together ever since.'

'That's wonderful. How much of a comfort it must be to have a friend such as that. One must be careful of the friends Harry and I have – certainly it would be foolish to trust them with a life.' She smiled. 'Business friendships, you understand.'

'Hansi teaches sport to Swiss children. He's a better climber than me – well, he has more practice. And more opportunity. He's good enough for a Six.'

She shook her head to indicate incomprehension.

'I'm boring you,' I said.

But she insisted that I explain, so I told her about the Welzenbach grading system, and how Hansi was in the highest group. 'We'll have to get back to your lesson, though,' I said; 'you're paying me to teach, not to tell my life story.'

For several minutes I explained some basic principles of German grammar, illustrating my points by sentences from *Faust*.

Quite suddenly, with a directness I did not expect, she said – 'Mr Tinnion, do you belong there? More than you do here?'

'What?'

'Where you grew up?'

'Switzerland?' I thought for a few seconds. 'Yes,' I said. 'Yes, I do.'

'I thought so,' she said, a little smugly. 'Are your parents still there?'

'No,' I said. The failure of the mill, and the sudden decline in our fortunes, had put rifts between us that would take years to heal. I had no intention of seeing them for a few years yet. 'They live in Brighton,' I said.

She pulled a face, as if this was surely a fall from grace. 'It must be a beautiful country. You're happy there.' She said this as an unquestionable statement. I did not disagree.

'It has a certain stolidity, Mrs Swarbrick. The Swiss have a chequered past, but now they're a self-aware, stable country. I'd rather go there than to its neighbours. All of Europe is volatile at the moment.'

'Germany, you mean?'

'And Italy, Spain. They may have burned books in Switzerland in the past, but not any more. And there's a certain liberalism there now, which makes even its more feudal aspects – franchise, for instance – seem preferable to the alternatives next door.'

I was trying to impress her. I stopped, and looked at her. Her gaze was quizzical, partly amused. I lowered my eyes, and coughed.

'*German,*' I said, to indicate we should get back to the subject.

But I was remembering how, as boys, Hansi and I had gone to a travelling cinema to see a film about climbers. The screen and projector had been set up in an old barn, and we had sat on wooden benches to watch the film. The barn smelled of old resin. Some of the planking had become warped, so angled shafts of light cut through the gloom like sun through high, narrow windows until all the gaps were stuffed up with sacking.

The film was called *Der Heilige Berg*. When it had ended Hansi and I ran out into the sunlight, among the tethered horses and parked bicylces. We had each fallen in love with Leni Riefenstahl, we said; here was an actress who could climb, ski, and brave real danger. And we fantasised how we, as men, would make hazardous journeys into the unknown, and be rewarded with riches, fame, and the love of a beautiful woman.

By late afternoon we had reached the cave. It was a disappointment. We had believed it to be comfortably large, but it was little more than a deep, dark recess, able to accommodate us and our equipment, but nothing else. We stored our rucksacks and went ahead to reconnoitre the vertical crack. It seemed a long time since I had called down to Hansi that I would lead as far as that; now it was becoming obvious that we would have to postpone our attempt until the morning.

We squatted opposite each other like yogis and began to prepare our meal. The first thing Hansi drew from his sack, however, was a screw-top jar full of clear fluid. Inside floated two beetles, upside-down, their wing cases slightly open. 'I found them just above Friendly Ledge,' he explained. 'Perhaps they're common; I can't tell. Still, young Bruno may find them interesting.'

'I didn't know you were doing this,' I said.

He laughed and held the jar between us, peering at me through its curvatures. His face became distorted, like the reflection in a funfair mirror. 'He's just a child. I don't think he fully understands why I can't overload myself with bottles and come back to him with different species collected at different heights, each bottle labelled exactly. I'll collect what I can, though.'

'Did Max ask you to do this?'

'That's right.' He placed the bottle safely on a ledge.

'We said we wouldn't bring anything that wasn't essential.'

'True. But what is more essential than the enthusiasm of the young?' He took off his gloves and began to rub his fingers. 'Max says I must be a good teacher.'

'What does he know about it?'

'He has connections, Ernst. Lots of them. He's a very useful man to know.' He grinned as he became boyishly confidential. 'He even knows an old flame of ours.'

I could not understand what he meant.

'You must remember,' he joked. 'The woman we would have dedicated our lives to?'

I had set up the heater by now, and was warming some stew. 'You mean a certain actress?' I asked.

His smile was impish. 'She has moved on; she's a director now. Max met her in Berlin. She's the perfect woman, it seems. Or so the government think. They have given her whatever she wants to make her Olympic film. Max says it will take her two years just to cut it.'

'Really,' I said, stirring the stew.

'Max says he prefers to work with a still camera. The results can be arranged much more quickly.'

'Help me make the tea, will you?' I asked, a little curtly.

Within a few minutes we were eating hot, meaty stew and drinking tea. I noticed that Hansi gripped his bowl and mug as if he needed to warm his hands on them.

'Trouble?' I asked, as casually as I could.

He shook his head quickly. 'A tingle, no more. Ever since Kurz –' He stopped. 'A fine view,' he said after a while.

'Yes,' I said.

Droplets of water gathered on the roof then dripped from it. Below us the whole valley was in full shadow, with only the high peaks still lit by the dying sun.

'Ernst,' Hansi began, then stopped.

I waited.

'Will you marry her?' he asked.

I filled my mouth with too large a spoonful of food so that I had time to consider my answer. 'I don't think so. Divorces in England are difficult and lengthy. And they cost a lot of money. I don't know what will happen.'

'Max knows about you, you know.'

I feigned indifference. 'Does he?'

'He must have suspected all the time. He asked me straight out. What could I do but tell him? I didn't say much. In fact, I told him very little.'

'There's not much to know, Hansi.'

'They say a soldier should always have a sweetheart, but never a wife. A wife, children – they tie a man down, and make him

38

incapable of fulfilling his destiny. Only later should he devote himself to a wife and family.'

'I'm not thinking of family life.'

'Max says that is what all women want.'

'Jean as well? That's a laugh.'

'That's what he says.'

The snow peaks became stained with rose, and a sudden, gigantic moon came up into a sky tinged with violet. Inside our cave it became inky black but for the pale, hesitant light from the heater.

'I wonder, Ernst, if you have found the woman for you. Max doubts it. And I can see that you have changed. You've become more serious. I do not even know if, in your heart of hearts, you wanted to make this climb.'

I said nothing.

'Perhaps it will be our last,' he said; 'even the best of partnerships must end sometime.'

3

NEXT TO THE PENSION WAS A BARN. HANSI HAD ALREADY STORED his motorcycle in it, and that afternoon we laid out our equipment in front of its doors as if for a kit inspection. Hansi had drawn up a list, and now he checked off the items one by one. Jean stood with us. She was wearing a loose, full skirt and a short-sleeved blouse. For much of the time she had her arms folded. She was fascinated by the array, and asked Hansi questions she had previously asked me. When I protested that I had already given her answers she laughed. 'I like to hear Hansi's opinions,' she told me, 'even if they are the same as yours.'

Hansi, flattered and charmed by Jean, took great care with his explanations, and made them as full as he could.

'These are the best,' he said, holding up a crampon.

'They look like torture implements,' Jean mused.

He did not realise that she already knew what they were. 'They fasten on the soles,' he said, 'and lace together across the boot tops. Now that we have these, the days of *tricouni* soles are over.' He tapped the metal with his fingernail. 'These are twelve-pointers, like Grivel used, with lobsterclaw spikes. The steel is the best that there is, and the curvature of the rim, the length and angle of the spikes are judged exactly. We can hold our own weight on vertical ice with these.'

Jean took one from him, pressed a spike lightly with her thumb, then passed it back. 'It will take ages to fasten them tightly enough.' I walked behind Hansi and, when he could not see me, I raised my hands to show that I could not understand why she asked. When Hansi bent down to show her how they

40

fastened, she put her tongue out at me as soon as she could not be seen.

'The hemp laces shrink when they are wet, so the fit will be as tight as possible. Believe me, the crampons are a gift.' This time he used the German word, *steigeisen*.

'And all these?' she asked.

'My iceaxe, and Ernest's. Pick them up, if you wish, and feel how well-balanced they are. Metal pegs, pitons – these are best for rock, these for ice, and there is a hammer we shall use for them. This is a *karabiner* –' He looked at me.

'Snap-links,' I said.

He nodded rapidly, as if he should have known. 'German words, Italian, French – the language of climbing is international, yes?'

She nodded. 'Yes,' she said, drily.

'These are a new design – Herzog used them on the Dreizink-enspitze. Our sleeping bags, which have been adapted from Zdarsky sacks. A lantern which folds – like this, you see? – and, to protect us from the sun, Crème Séchehaye. It is easy to get sunburn if the ice is reflective. These ropes are the best Italian hemp, and here is our altimeter.'

Jean pointed out a knitted woollen helmet. 'Back in England, we call those balaclavas.'

'Ernst taught me that word a long, long time ago. Yes, we have to wear them. Wool keeps the warmth in – and corduroy,viyella, whipcord.'

'And those are your knives, and your goggles – for glare?'

'Yes.'

'And these are your cooking utensils. They look like aluminium.'

'I have already cleaned them. Those stains should not be removed. It is the white spots which are dangerous; you have to clean those out with carbonate of soda, and rinse them with very weak nitric acid. Aluminium is light. That is its main advantage,

Jean. But you cannot leave tea or spirits in it for more than a day.'

'Before we begin,' I said, 'we'll pack some food that is high in energy and won't take up much space. That means we'll go up by the east ridge and store it on the summit.'

'We'll do that tomorrow,' Hansi said.

'Tomorrow? Ernest, you can't go tomorrow.'

She spoke quite firmly, like an affronted schoolmistress. Her arms were still folded, and I noticed one finger repeatedly tapping the crook of the other arm in a discharge of nervousness.

I could not understand why she had spoken in such a way. 'Why not?' I asked, colouring slightly as if I was her pupil. Out of the corner of my eye I saw Hansi deliberately turn away to rearrange some equipment, as if he did not wish to be drawn into our disagreement.

'You promised me,' she said firmly.

'Promised you what?'

'To take me to the glacier.' She stared directly at me, daring me to contradict her. I had mentioned the glacier, and said we should go there sometime, but had never specified when and I certainly had made no promise. 'I've spoken to Clara Seematter,' Jean continued, 'she says we may borrow the horse and trap. The day after that, and the one after that as well, they have to use it.'

I looked across at Hansi, who had straightened. I waited for him to say something, but he did not. I wanted to tell him that I was innocent, but was certain that Jean's contradiction would be vehement.

'I'm sorry, Hansi,' she said, suddenly oversweet towards him, 'but it looks as if your little expedition will have to wait.'

'A day will make no difference,' he said. But Hansi had always been a stickler for routine and schedule, and I knew that he was unhappy at this new development.

'I'm sorry,' Jean said again, but there was no contrition in her voice, and when she walked once more around our equipment there was the spring of victory in her step.

'And we shall have to move all this up to the hut,' Hansi said. 'Tell me, Ernest, after tomorrow you are free, aren't you?' The sarcasm was light but effective.

'Of course.' I looked across at Jean, who smiled at me like a nurse to a patient. 'After tomorrow, I belong completely to the climb,' I said.

He nodded, and picked up the altimeter, tapping it gently on one side. 'How does it work?' Jean asked, as if there were no tensions at all between us.

About ten minutes after this, Max Volkwein's car drew up beside the pension. Bruno sat beside him, his face tightening as soon as he saw us. I saw Max whisper in his ear, and then he stepped casually from the car and sauntered across to us. Bruno did not move for a while, then he got out of the car and began to pick objects from his haversack and arrange them on the running-board.

'My nephew collects everything,' Max said. 'I tell him he must be more selective. Why, he would strip a whole area of its wildlife if he could.' He smiled tolerantly, and all the while his eyes flicked between the three of us. 'I see that you are holding a little exhibition, gentlemen. It *is* just the gentlemen, isn't it? Wherever these two are going, Mrs Tinnion, it looks as if you will be staying behind.'

'An upland stroll, Herr Volkwein,' Hansi said.

'Really? And there are such magnificent faces around here. This equipment would be good enough for them. But of course, both of you know that.'

Hansi and I both knew he was waiting for our exchange of glances. We did not look at each other.

'We must have a little relaxation every so often,' Hansi responded cheerfully. 'It does a man no good if he is always pushing himself to the limit.'

'Ah, but it is the limit which matters, do you not agree?'

We did not answer. Max looked round. I was hoping he would leave, but he showed no sign of doing so. Instead he behaved like a man who knew a secret, and was considering whether or not he should reveal it.

'So, Mrs Tinnion,' he continued, 'you will be left behind? Is this not a strange honeymoon?'

'It's all right,' Jean said, 'I was expecting them to climb.'

'Of course, I realise that it will not be a surprise to you.'

'It was arranged before we left England.'

Max nodded. At last it seemed as if he was about to leave, but after taking a few steps away from us he turned as if a thought had suddenly struck him.

'I am a very fit person, gentlemen. I have to be. You should know, I think, that I have been on mountains myself – nothing approaching your standard, of course, but it is possible that I may be able to help you.'

Neither Hansi nor I responded.

'A two-man team has preparations which are tedious and perhaps arduous,' he went on. 'They could be eased by the assistance of someone else.'

'Perhaps,' Hansi said, grudgingly.

'I am just talking about preparations, you understand.'

We stared at each other for what seemed like several seconds. No one spoke.

Max laughed as if he had just discovered a private joke. 'We are pretending with each other, aren't we? I believe you have a certain goal, and you suspect me of knowing this. And you are worried about what I may do. You should not be concerned. I know about your sport, I know about its ethics and its duels. You may consider me knowledgeable but discreet. At the very least, you have my sympathy and my admiration. But, if you wish, you may have my assistance.'

Before we could answer, he took a few steps further away and then paused again. He was like an actor making the most of an exit.

'I telephoned one of my contacts in the press today,' he said. His neutrality could not disguise his glee. 'I am a man who has to know many, many people. He is ready to leave Munich at any time. He knows that very soon, tomorrow, maybe today, there will be an attempt on another north wall.'

I could sense the tension in the air, even though Hansi and I maintained our nonchalant postures.

'Is that so?' I asked after a short while.

Max walked back towards us, bending his body forward as if we were all conspirators. 'I asked him about that,' he said, and pointed behind himself in the direction of the Versücherin. 'He tells me that the Italians will do it. Very soon. Bissolati has a six-man team which he has brought together especially for the purpose.'

He smiled, and began to walk back to the car again. Bruno gazed sullenly at him.

'Perhaps it will happen before my holiday is ended,' Max said. 'Perhaps I have arrived here at just the right time. Yes?'

With that he left, collecting Bruno and his samples on the way.

'Well?' I asked Hansi.

'I don't know. Is he telling the truth?'

'He could be.'

'He will be,' Jean said. 'He has no reason to lie.'

'No?' I asked. Jean had chosen to lie about the glacier; no doubt she had given herself a reason.

Hansi put his hands up to his chin. 'We are in danger, Ernst. Time is catching up with us. What do you know about this Volkwein?'

'Nothing much. He's confident, and something of a schemer.'

He nodded. 'I have met Bissolati. He's one of the best.'

'There's no sign of Bissolati. There are not even any rumours about him.'

'Ernst, there are no rumours about *us*, and we are going to climb the mountain very soon.'

He turned away and, apparently lost in thought, stood with his eyes fixed on the arrangement of equipment.

Hansi and I had believed our equations to be clear and precise, but now Jean and Max had entered them, and they had become less manageable, possibly volatile. Hansi and I were experienced, strong, capable. We understood and trusted each other, but now our friendship was being changed by the presence of others.

It worried me that our motives were so transparent to Max, and it worried me further that he wished to be part of our attempt. And I was disturbed because Jean had lied, and I could not understand why. She had talked about glaciers when we had been in England, but when I had mentioned the subject a few days ago she had not reacted. Perhaps her sense of isolation was fuelling a kind of jealousy, and now she felt compelled to assert some kind of influence. I resented this. Our false marriage had not yet settled into a permanent understanding, and yet she was acting as if it had.

Quite suddenly I saw that everything around me was unstable. The future had shrunk so that I could see no more than a couple of days ahead. Beyond that it was so unpredictable, so formless that it could not even be considered.

I realised, with a queasy, sickening force, that within a few days I could be dead.

That afternoon Hansi and I walked to the top of the hill where he had camped. Near to the chestnut tree we stopped. Otto had lent us his small telescope; we set it up on its tripod and took turns to study the Versücherin through it.

The wall possessed one place name only, and that was Friendly Ledge. The origins of the name were obscure, although Otto had

claimed that, during the last century, a world-famous mountaineer (Whymper, he thought) had passed through the valley
and remarked that the ledge was the only friendly feature on the
entire wall.

Beyond that we had to invent names. Most were easy, and as
Hansi took us step by step through our intended route we could
name the long column, the first icefield, the cave, the vertical
crack. One name – the flume – was ironic, for Hansi said that it
looked as if it had been engineered to carry water from the higher
slopes. Last of all, just below the summit, was the great ice plate
that sat at the very top of the wall. There was no way of avoiding
it, and it seemed that we would head towards it like victims
offering themselves for sacrifice. Even the ridges of black rock
which ran across it had an ugly, menacing appearance.

Hansi had brooded for a long time on this last stage of the
climb. 'It's like a trap,' he said, 'like a spider's web.'

From then onwards, it became the web.

Beyond the web lay the summit, hidden from our eyes by the
towering perspectives of the cliffs.

We discussed again, in fine detail, the techniques we would
use, the stores we would carry, the bivouacs we would have to
make. All the time we tried to speak lightly of the most dangerous
parts of the climb. When, at last, we had discussed as much as we
could, we sat together under the tree and reminisced about other
climbs we had made, and the people we had met.

For some time we could laugh, but Hansi gradually became
sombre. 'Too many of us have died, Ernst,' he said. 'The list is
very long. And even Welzenbach is dead now.'

'And Toni Kurz.'

He nodded. 'I met him for the first time earlier this year. He was
full of confidence, and talked about his partnership with Hinterstoisser. Rainer and Angerer I had heard of, but never met.'

I said nothing, but rested my hand on the gleaming barrel of the
telescope.

'No one should be allowed to hang like that,' Hansi went on. 'He was just out of reach. We could do nothing.'

I had read the reports in Otto's scrapbook. After one of them was injured, the team had begun to descend the Eiger. They were within earshot of rescuers when the last, fatal fall happened. No one saw it, but only Kurz had been left alive. Hinterstoisser had vanished; Rainer had frozen to death; Angerer hung from the rope below Kurz, strangled where he had fallen.

For hour after hour the rescuers had struggled to reach Kurz in his impossible position. At last he managed to cut himself free of Angerer's body, and gradually he had descended the rock in a sling fastened to the rope by a snap-link. All the time Hansi and the others urged him on, shouting encouragement and telling him he had only a few metres to go before he reached them.

But the knot had become fast in the snap-link, and he could go no further. His left arm was a useless frozen club, and his face had grown purple with fatigue and frostbite. His voice, which had been clear, was almost unintelligible. Doggedly he tried to loosen the knot with his teeth. Just below him welcoming arms, including Hansi's, were held out.

'We were willing him on,' Hansi said, 'If we could have helped him, we would. But we needed to have the wings of angels.'

He was silent for a short while.

'Quite suddenly,' he continued, 'he said *I'm finished*. They were the only clear words he had spoken for some time. And then his body tipped forward, and he was dead. The sling was hanging just beyond our reach.'

We sat together and watched the shadows grow on the Versücherin wall.

'If I thought I could help things by never climbing again, I would do it,' Hansi said. 'But I can see no point in relinquishing all this. If I never set another foot on another mountain, it would not save another life.'

'Except perhaps your own. Or mine.'

'You think there is a purpose in giving up?'

'There's no shame in admitting defeat.'

'I mean completely, not just tactically.'

'Not just yet, no. But if Toni Kurz had decided to give it up, or Hinterstoisser, or Welzenbach –'

'All things must come to an end, and often we do not know what that will be. If I had not watched Toni die, I would not have had the determination to climb the Versücherin wall.'

'No?'

Hansi clenched his fist and held it over his chest. 'His death was like a fuse, Ernst. It has set off a chain of events which we are a part of. The culmination, the achievement will be when we both stand on the pinnacle of the wall. I know this will happen. I can feel it in my blood.' He looked at me closely. 'Don't you feel this, too?'

I laughed. 'I've never been as visionary as you, Hansi.'

Concerned, he took me by the shoulder. 'But you must have something – a kind of confidence, a belief that we'll succeed?'

'Why yes,' I said, 'of course I have.'

Hansi had always been certain, always been determined about mountains. Among them he had found his true purpose in life. In his pursuit of achievement he had been able to avoid all the difficulties and uncertainties of the ordinary; instead he chose to face the dangerous, the pure.

As a mountaineer, Hansi was exceptional. He was steadfast and decisive, and followed his strategy with a military single-mindedness and pragmatism. If we ever came across a difficult problem, it was Hansi who made the choice.

And yet, among the life of the valleys, Hansi always shied away from confrontation. He was so eager to avoid dissension that he even took on the characteristics of those around him. It was not that he was a hypocrite or a liar; on the contrary, he was one of the most honest men I had ever met. But he was easily influenced, and often he was malleable.

He must have been aware of this, although in his early years that awareness may have been unconscious. As a child he had dreamed up a familiar. He had called this imaginary friend Rudi. It was Rudi who always sympathised with Hansi, always supported him. Often, when Hansi was uncertain or alone, Rudi would take him through flights of fancy in which he and Hansi were adventurous, successful, and always together.

Until he met me, Rudi was Hansi's constant companion. It was not until much later, of course, that I learned about him, although, with hindsight, I should have detected his fading presence at our early meetings. When Hansi finally did confess, it was as if, by telling me about Rudi, he was initiating me into the most grave of all secrets.

By then Hansi had begun to mirror my attitudes, my beliefs. And yet, of the two of us, in many ways he was the stronger. He deferred to me in many areas, for he believed me to be more intelligent and, since I was a foreigner, to have a wider experience of the outside world.

With women, for instance, Hansi was curiously reticent and often uneasy, even though his boyish good looks and athleticism drew them to him. He was comfortable enough with older women, or the wives of friends; it was as if he feared that free women could trap him, compromise him because he did not possess the ability to lie. His devotion and faith was for the mountains, and for those of us who shared his passion. He would never have been able to flee his country with someone like Jean.

The next day I took Jean to the glacier. It had been a few years since I had driven a pony and trap, but the Seematters' animal was docile and biddable, and after a mile I was comfortable and in control. Clara had made us a picnic lunch in a wicker basket, and for the occasion Jean was wearing a checked shirt and shorts that were turned up just above the knee.

As we headed up the valley the fields began to narrow and there were fewer and fewer farms. The mountains drew together more closely, and often the woods grew right down to the valley floor so that we had to drive through their shadow. Sometimes, too, we passed huge boulders that had been dumped centuries ago by the retreating ice, and at one point we passed a roadside crucifix made from welded metal spars. It stood among mossy tree-stumps with saplings shooting from them, as if it marked the site of a fatal accident.

Once we had passed over a wooden bridge which spanned a low river we entered an unbroken forest. The air was full of tiny flies and smelled of resin, and all we could see were the trunks of pines, an infinity of green needles, and, above our heads, a ragged band of sky. The road surface worsened, and I slowed the horse, but I could not avoid all the potholes and the trap jarred as we bounced across them. Beside the road were curls of bark, piles of sawdust, and smashed branches. I remembered the visits I had made to my father's sawmill. The whine of the saws and the rhythm of the motors had always carried to us across the meadows, so that I associated them with prosperity and stability. Inside, the mill smelled of shavings, there was always straw-coloured dust in the air, stacks of raw planking encroaching on every doorway, conveyor belts slapping, and from the seasoning vats came a tang as sharp as the sea. Once I had gone to the mill and seen a man standing, quite casually, beside a divided metal ramp which fed a still-turning vertical saw. He had wound a cloth around one hand, and the sawdust at his feet was spotted with blood. One of the foreman took me by the shoulders and shepherded me away. Only later did I learn that the man had lost two of his fingers as he pressed a spar against the cutting edge. It was not a thing which should give me bad dreams, my father told me; such men understood the hazards of their work, and the loss of a finger or two was but little. I did not think of this remark as callous until I was much older.

After a while the forest thinned, and we stopped in the middle of a strange, alien landscape the colour of ash and stone. Around the road were a series of sculpted hillocks with geometrical edges, like stylised waves, and hunched, uneven columns taller than a man. 'Rubble and grit,' I said, 'left here when the ice retreated. These are unusual. The wind must make them like that.'

It was true. The wind and rain had chiselled the hillocks like soft wood. The mounds, towers, facets, inclines had been curved, hollowed and turned as if by a coherent shaping force. On their surfaces could be seen fluted, repetitive patterns, like hard sand marked by a current. Jean placed her hands against one of the surfaces, and when she took them away I could see that they were marked with pieces of grit and tiny pebbles. She dashed her palms clean.

Now the track came to resemble a drove road, and the trap bounced across it uncomfortably. Boulders scabbed with lichen and ringed with clumps of fern stood on either side of us, and the trees and shrubs were sparse and undernourished. Then we came to a smooth, springy turf, the way cleared, and we were facing the glacier.

The glacier was cream and grey and lined with greenish-brown striations. Behind it the mountains rose in a configuration of peaks. The glacier ended in a high, raggedly convex wall, and from its base a milky-grey river ran through fanned-out mounds of rock and gravel.

'I expected it to be white,' Jean said, a trace of disappointment in her voice.

'Come on,' I said, 'I'll tether the horse and we'll walk down to it. Is it so much of an anti-climax?'

'No. This just isn't what I expected, that's all.'

I took the wicker basket and led the way along the slope towards the mouth of the glacier. Jean followed me, sometimes holding my hand if the way was steep. 'During the ice ages this glacier carved its way down the entire valley,' I said. 'All this debris was carried along by it. It cut away the north face of the Versücherin as well. Erosion did the rest. Now it grows or shrinks a little, year by year. Only by a few yards, though. That's why there are few trees here – the climate is too hostile, the soil too thin. Look at this rock here. See those lines? That's where ice has passed over, scoring this with another rock embedded within it.'

'This is all quite harsh and bleak. I thought it would be more – well, more fairytale.'

The glacier wall was grimy and sparkling. Around its base, between beds of shingle and sand, streams of pearlescent water bubbled across shallows or gathered in opaque pools. We picked our way across spits of debris which gave beneath the heel, and I pointed to the underside of the ice cliff where there was a series of dark hollows, like the nestholes of gigantic birds.

The temperature fell further, as if the ice fuelled its own dissolution by sucking warmth from the air. The glacier walls flashed with rivulets of meltwater. 'Can we go closer?' she asked.

I hesitated.

'Those are caves, aren't they? Is it safe to go inside?'

'Sometimes it is.' The truth was that I did not know. I had crossed glaciers, but never before had I investigated one so threateningly decayed. 'We'll go a little closer, if it pleases you,' I said.

We trod gingerly across two areas of shining pebbles. Numbingly cold water soaked upwards through my boots, and I wished that I had worn my pair for climbing. I could see that Jean, too, was cold, but she would never admit it. Inside the caves I could see a chilling greenish dark. 'This is close enough,' I warned.

'We can go closer, Ernest. We can go *into* one. Look, the ice above that one has been shaped like an arch. The weight above it flows round the cave, so you can see there's no danger.' She grabbed my arm excitedly. 'Let's go inside.'

I hesitated.

'Do it for me,' she asked.

The cavern was wide and ran back a surprisingly long way, but we had to stoop to enter it. To go further we had to remain crouched. The floor was slippery bedrock, littered with loose pebbles, and the roof was a dripping forest of icicles. Within the ice there were dark studs of rock.

We were several yards inside the cave when we had to stop. The passageway ceased at a bulging wall of darkly shining ice. There was just enough light to see each other. I was balanced on my haunches, with my fingers on rock which had been ground perfectly.

'Is this as close to the heart as we can get?' she asked. Her voice sounded both constricted and hollow. I thought of a fruit held firmly and scooped empty of its pulp.

'Yes.' My breath misted in front of me.

'It's as cold as a grave. No, colder.' She paused, then said, 'Do you remember what you told me once, Ernest? You told me about a dead man coming out of a glacier.' Her voice was sharp, and her eyes had widened like a cat's in the gloom.

'There are always stories like that.'

She put a hand on my face. I winced because her touch was so cold. 'Perhaps that could happen to you, Ernest. You'll vanish from my sight, and I'll think you have run away. But years later, an old woman, I'll be brought to see your body lying at the bottom of a glacier. You'll be just as you are now – hair, fingernails, even the little cut you made while shaving this morning. They'll know who you are by the papers in your pockets, but I'll have to come along to identify the lover of my youth.'

I felt the chill spread through my belly and heart. 'Our climb is nowhere near the glacier.'

'But I suspect you would think of that as a marvellous fate. Wouldn't you? To never grow old, to always look as you do now, to be carried along in silence and peace. It would be majestic, a fitting end.'

'I hadn't thought of it.'

We were silent. I expected to hear the roof groan, to have a gate of ice crash down to block the entrance, but there was only the dribbling, trickling sound of water.

Jean picked up a pebble, then began to sort through them. I remained still, my fingers on the eerily smooth bedrock. Finally she selected one which fitted comfortably into her palm. It was in the shape of a flattened oval. 'I'll keep this as a memento,' she said. And then, quite suddenly, her nerve seemed to fail her and she grabbed my shirt at the shoulder. 'Let's get out of here,' she said.

I led the way back to the light. She followed me, reaching out and touching me several times like a child afraid of becoming lost. Once we were outside she held my hand and would not let go, even though the sun dazzled and everything around us became warmer. Her lips were partly open and appeared swollen. The cold, I supposed.

We walked across the basin of the glacier, crossing fans and hillocks of gravel, stones, clay. Heat mounted around us.

The further we were from the ice wall, the less bare the landscape became. Tufts of vegetation could be seen in the crevices of boulders, and moss spilled across the sides of rocks. Hoverflies rose and fell around us. Soon we were in the trough of the valley, with grassy slopes rising from the chalky river. The slopes were crisscrossed by narrow tracks, as if the soil had become unstable and was slipping towards the water in great scales of turf.

We quickly reached a level area of ground which was carpeted with flowers with pink or yellow heads. Large rocks littered the area, thick green spears of grass sprouting from beneath them. We sat down and I opened the haversack. Folded on the top of its contents was a German-language magazine.

I looked at Jean, puzzled. 'Did you buy this?'

'Max lent it to me just as we were leaving. He wants it back, though.'

I passed it across to her but did not look at it. When I found our bottle of white wine I walked with it down the gravel bank, which crunched beneath me. I placed the bottle in the river and lodged it with stones so that it would not be carried away. I splashed water on my face. It was still icily cold, and stung. When I pushed my hands through my hair I could feel the strands sticking together in damp spikes.

Jean had turned so that she could leaf through the magazine, which she had spread on the turf. I lay down beside her, looking up into the sky, then closed my eyes. The grass was springy and rich, and all around me was the smell of growth. Beneath me I could feel the massed looseness and tension of stalks, petals, leaves. I opened my eyes slightly. The sun lanced across them, so that when I closed them tightly I saw an unreal landscape of dark silver and drifting geometries.

'Max is in here,' Jean said.

'Oh?'

'He has a portfolio of photographs of the Olympics.'

An insect buzzed in my ear, its noise magnified and persistent before it moved away. I could still hear the patterns of the river.

'Are they good?' I asked.

'Very.'

I could hear the pages turn slowly, as if she was studying each one. After a few minutes I rolled over and lay beside her so that I, too, could read the magazine. She was looking at an advertisement for clothes. 'Turn back,' I said, 'I'd like to see them.'

'You didn't sound interested.'

'Come on,' I said, annoyed.

She turned back the pages. Max's photographs framed the athletes against skies like dark silk. Frozen in time, their bodies caught in velocity and torque, they looked like visions of gods.

'They're impressive, aren't they?'

'Yes,' I admitted grudgingly.

'They all look so strong, so appealing. Even in defeat.'

'What you must remember is that these have been selected from a lot of others that weren't anything like as good. Look at the expressions on these people's faces – they show triumph, determination, courage. There must have been some where the athletes looked ugly, or stupid, or just plain ordinary.'

'Ernest, I believe you're jealous.'

She said it in a teasing voice, so I bit my tongue.

After a few minutes I retrieved the bottle. Jean handed me a corkscrew; I opened it as the label turned to pulp and slid away in my hand. We ate hard-boiled eggs, cheese, ham, spiced sausage, and bread that Clara had baked that morning.

'You're sulking,' Jean said.

'No I'm not.'

'*Are* you jealous of Max?'

'Of course not,' I scoffed. 'Why should I be?'

'He gives the impression of knowing what he wants to do.'

'And I don't?'

'Not in the long term, no. All your goals are immediate ones, no more than a few weeks away.'

I was astonished that she should think of me in such a way. It was she who was a creature of impulse, not me. Everything I did was calculated; I had even worried that I was, if anything, a little too cold in my relationships with others.

'Oh,' she went on, 'I don't mean that you're completely short-sighted. It's just that, once beyond the immediate, your thoughts become abstract, woolly, more like a daydream than anything else. Did you seriously think about the Versücherin until quite recently? I mean in a real, concentrated, practical sense? Or perhaps you have Hansi to do that for you?'

'If it hadn't been for you we would have been ascending the east ridge right now,' I countered. 'I never made a promise to bring you here today. You lied about that.'

'I wanted to see this. And I wanted to come here with *you*.'

'There would have been time after the climb.'

'Ernest, after the climb things will be different. I don't know how, but they will be. You both want to be heroes, and perhaps that's what you will become. But other things could happen – I pray that they won't, but I have to consider that possibility.' She paused for a while. 'That's why I lied. I wanted us to have one last day together. Just you and I.' I must have looked perplexed, because, quite suddenly, she laughed. 'Ernest, you have a curious innocence about you. If this were a pastoral idyll –' She stopped and looked at me. I nodded. 'If this were like some of those paintings you showed me, then you would be the shepherd, handsome and unworldly, and I would be the huntress.'

Yes, I thought, beautiful, alabaster-skinned, with the morality of the divine.

Jean pushed her hand through her hair, took another drink, and studied me. 'I don't think you ever really got over your childhood. That's where I have an advantage over you. I have nothing to be sentimental about.'

And I thought of the things I had told her so that my youth would seem rich, unusual, enviable. How Hansi had shown me that he could feed cattle with handfuls of caked salt, which made them so tame that he could pull their horns, grasp their tongues, tug their lips. How, at the end of summer, men returned from the high pastures behind cattle garlanded with flowers, and were judged by the beards they had grown, and how sometimes beermugs were pounded so hard that they shattered on the wooden tables. How Hansi and I went to a yodelling competition that went on until the early hours, and how we walked from a muggy, tobacco-thick air into a night that was chill, crisp, and full of falling stars. I told her how marmots whistled, and yellow saxifrage grew high on the slopes, and how more than once, on mountains, I had looked down to see my own shadow cast on clouds below me, and how it was edged by the colours of the rainbow. And how we once discovered the ruins of an old castle, jumbles of stone that were overgrown by moss and swallowed by pines. The flagstones of the great hall still made a clearing in the greenery, and we had imagined men in armour seated in front of huge fire, with a pig roasting over it on a spit.

I had not told her, however, that we had taken two girls there. We were fourteen, no more. Somewhat reluctantly, Hansi showed them trees that had been frosted by *elfenbecher* fungus. An owl slid past in eerie daylight silence, and where the drainage down the slopes was poor we discovered a clearing that was crowded from side to side with purple gentian. We had talked, giggled, clowned, and showed off shamelessly. Nothing else had happened, but it had been one of the happiest days I had ever spent.

I lay back and closed my eyes. 'Perhaps,' I told Jean.

We did not speak for several minutes.

'Ernest,' she said at last, 'what will happen to us?'

'Why do you ask such things, Jean? Can't you just live for the moment?'

'I can't afford to.'

'You shouldn't worry so much. Be content.'

'How can I be content?' Her voice sounded close to me, as if her mouth was only an inch from my ear.

'Really?' I asked. I was perturbed because I thought I had given her some sort of satisfaction.

'Oh, I've been happy, but that's different. Happiness might not last. I've never been *settled*, if that's what you mean. When I got married I remember thinking that somehow I had been sold short. It's difficult for women, Ernest. I don't think you understand that. Security and adventure pull us in different directions. You may think me impulsive, you may even think me irrational, but I have to do a certain amount of planning ahead.' She paused.

I could still hear the liquid riffling of the meltwater. 'What will happen to me if you are killed?' she asked at last.

I did not expect her to raise the question, even though I knew she must have considered it. 'It's bad luck to even talk about it,' I replied.

'I want a sensible answer, not one that dismisses the problem.'

'You expect me to worry about what happens to you after I die? Jean, I have enough on my mind. You don't realise what is involved in an assault like this. It consumes all your energy, and all your mind as well. Now please, let me have a little peace before we start. I can't afford to be distracted.'

When she spoke again, I could hear the hurt in her voice. 'Surely my life isn't a distraction for you?'

I dared not open my eyes. 'Please, Jean, don't say things like that.'

'Ernest, I've burned my boats. I can't return to Harry. My money is being spent, and I no longer have friends I could fall back on. I could be marooned here.'

I said nothing, but heard her turn away. After a short while I decided that I would embrace her, and tell her that I loved her, but by the time I sat up she had left me and was walking alone by the stream.

Otto came to meet us as soon as we returned. His walk was almost a swagger, and his face was set with a reined-in pride. As I got down from the trap he seized my hand and held it firmly. 'It's all right,' he said, 'your secret is safe with us.'

For a moment I thought that Hansi must have told him that Jean and I were not married, until the more obvious explanations hit me. He knew about the north wall.

'Hansi told you about the climb,' I said flatly.

He shook my hands as if working a pump, steadying my arm at the elbow with his other hand. 'I was proud to help them,' he said. 'I shall be proud to have helped you too, Herr Tinnion, when you and Herr Kirchner begin your climb. I will have been a part of history in the making.'

'I don't understand,' Jean said; 'what's happened?'

Otto finally let go of me and stepped back to nod heavily at the Versücherin. 'I have slept in the hut just a few hundred metres below the eastern col. The army used it in exercises – oh, twenty, thirty years ago. If Hansi and Max do not return tonight, they will rest there.' He slapped his hands together and rubbed them as if he were particularly pleased with his involvement.

'Jean,' I said, 'Max is doing what I was supposed to do. They've taken stores by the east ridge to bury within the summit cairn. Isn't that right, Otto?'

'He is a very fit man, he tells me. And certainly he is very keen to help in any way that he can. He even took Hansi into town to buy one or two things before they began.' Otto became confidential, and leaned forward. 'I understand he is very important, too. He knows many, *many* people in Germany.'

'He's a man who overestimates his own importance,' I said, 'and one who pushes his way into things that have nothing to do with him.'

Otto was puzzled. 'That cannot be true,' he insisted. 'He is a world-class photographer, and has tried many of the sports he has photographed. Athletes, swimmers, climbers feel honoured to sit for him.'

Jean interceded quickly. 'What about the boy?'

'Young Bruno? He is happy enough. Clara will take his meal to his room, because he prefers to eat there.'

'I see,' she said.

But she would not accept this. While I brooded over the new turn of events, she went to Max and Bruno's room.

Later she told me how she had found Bruno sitting on the floor among bottles, tiny boxes, traps, open books, engrossed in his rapidly expanding collection. Bird feathers were lined up on the bed and he had just blown the contents from an egg with a straw. Some butterflies were pinned in a case, and several large beetles in another. At first he was wary of her, but then, when she questioned him about his collection, he began to talk freely.

I sat in the corner of the dining room, preoccupied and alone, when Clara approached me. 'I am sorry,' she said, 'but Mrs Tinnion has found a new friend.'

I had been scarcely thinking of Jean.

'They are talking about all kinds of things,' she went on, smiling, 'plants and animals, what lives off what. And your wife has begun to tell Bruno about where you come from in England. He is such a shy boy, and has hardly said anything since he came here. Mrs Tinnion must be a special kind of person, to put him at his ease as she has done.'

'Yes.'

'She is eating in his room with him. She said you would not mind?'

I shook my head; of course I didn't mind. Besides, my thoughts were of Hansi and Max, the emergency stores buried, descending the east ridge as the sun sank.

At this hour the ridge was a sharp division between an undifferentiated greyness and a sky of luminous, darkening blue. Even if I sat at a telescope and trained it for a long time on the path I knew they would have to use, I knew there was no chance of seeing their two figures high, high on the mountain.

I thought, then, of the only time my friendship with Hansi had been seriously threatened. As boys we had an intense, exclusive relationship. We squabbled, of course, and insulted each other in a kind of ritual, but our enmities seldom lasted more than an hour. After that we were, again, the closest of friends.

Once, however, I returned from a lengthy stay in England to find that Hansi had taken up with another boy. I was surprised and insulted by this. The boy was uncouth, brutal, and sly. He had slit the throats of fledglings and blown up frogs with a straw, and rumour had it that he copulated freely with his younger sister. He was a strange, unsettling friend for Hansi, who seemed compromised and embarrassed by my return. For several uncomfortable days Hansi tried to mediate between us, but his chances of pleasing us both were hopeless. And, although I walked around with them, I felt betrayed by him, and would not co-operate.

Eventually his new friend became bored. He called us stupid, stick-in-the-muds, teacher's pets, and drifted away. Within a few days Hansi and I had resumed our friendship as if this interloper had never existed.

But I did not forget him, and for a long time afterwards I could recall, with precise clarity, the feelings of humiliation and self-pity that made me hate Hansi so much that I would have murdered him.

4

IT WAS STILL DARK. I WAS SO ALERT THAT, FOR A MOMENT OR TWO, I wondered if I had been asleep, for it seemed that I had lain awake all night thinking of Jean. Water dripped sullenly from the cave roof, and our sleeping bags were spotted with patches of ice the size and thickness of fingernails.

Hansi was already awake. We said nothing, but struggled into position so we could light the heater. In silence, we brewed more tea and stiffened it with sugar to give us energy. Hansi studied the altimeter, then showed it to me; the reading was the same as it had been the day before. Then he moved out of the cave, lantern in hand, and stood a little way up the face.

Quickly I scribbled a note on a scrap of paper. It was my name, Jean's, the date, and our height on the Versücherin. I folded the paper, placed it in a tobacco tin I had picked up at the Seematters', and wedged it at the back of the cave.

Hansi slithered down, dimmed the lantern, and pointed out across the valley. Above the far mountains the sky was dove-grey. 'No time to waste,' he said.

We moved out on to bare rock, and within a few feet stood at the base of the crack. I paid out the rope as Hansi wormed his way upwards. All was quiet except for the hammering as Hansi drove supports into the rock.

'What condition?' I shouted.

'It angles outwards. Most will hold, but there are rotted sections. Keep out of the way.'

I moved across while several pieces of stone came bouncing down the open funnel as he swept them clear. I could only see a dim, foreshortened view of him. From far below came the clamour of a hundred or more rooks, and I knew that they were rising from their roosts just before the dawn. I coughed, spat out mucus, and looked towards the east.

After a few minutes I heard the click of a spring clip, as distinctive as the noise of a rifle bolt. 'Slings?' I called, but Hansi's reply was drowned in a shower of debris as he cleared the pitch. The light strengthened all the time.

It took another half hour for Hansi to be free from the top of the crack. I passed up the rucksacks by rope, and then began to follow his route, recovering what I could of the equipment as I swung on the end of the rope. Harsh and bright, the sun rose directly on to the face, but within the crack I still laboured upwards in darkness and frost.

The exit from the crack was a platform broad enough to stand on. As soon as I joined him Hansi gave me an encouraging smile. 'It's going well,' he said. Then, his expression altering, he added, 'It's disappointingly easy so far, but the rest will try us.'

Now we traversed the base of a sheer precipice. It had neither shelter nor foothold, and along its upper ridge was a bulbous lip of ice. All the time, afraid that the sun would loosen it, we glanced up, and I thought that perhaps it was from here that the ice had fallen to where we had passed it on the first stage of our climb. But nothing moved apart from a few thin streams of water which dribbled from its edge.

Soon we had passed the end of the cliff, where it had shattered into crumbling pillars, and we rested by some glazed and treacherous rocks beside the first icefield. I wondered if we were already being watched, but the angle of the sun was not yet right for us to be able to pick up the telltale flashes of light bounced from telescope lenses.

Hansi continued to lead across the outcrop, axing the glaze so that our footholds would be more secure. It fell and smashed with a delicate tinkling sound. At the far side he waited. I passed the rucksacks over on a snap-link, then crossed the outcrop myself.

At the icefield's edge we assessed our position, then decided that we must follow the planned route and go straight across. This was tedious rather than dangerous, although all the time I was aware of the giddy slide into nothingness. I chopped and kicked my way to the end of a rope, shards of ice skittering down the incline, then hammered in an ice peg and fed the rope through a clip slipped into its eye. 'I'll cut a shelf,' I shouted back to Hansi as he stood at the edge of the outcrop. He nodded as if a response in words was unnecessary.

The icefield was shadowy and, although the surface did not have the hardness that I would find higher up the mountain, I could feel my fingers, and later my toes, begin to lose heat. Nevertheless I was quite content, perched here thousands of feet above the rest of the world. At each blow of the axe the ice shuddered and parted in crystalline sprays, and thick plates came free, accelerating downwards with a gritty slither until they were out of earshot. When I had finished Hansi came across to join me on the rough platform.

'I should have been a builder,' I joked.

'Good,' he said, 'as a reward, you may build another.'

It took us three ropes until we neared the far side, and on the last stretch I came across half a dozen butterflies scattered unmoving across the ice. They had not been damaged in any way, but were fastened to the surface as if feeding from it. I stopped, took my weight on my axe, and picked up the nearest one. Its wings were the colour of tropical seas, and were dusted with ice crystals. If lifted easily away, but was as brittle as a creature made from glass. I held it in my hand, half expecting to see it revive, but it was completely still, the antennae as stiff as wire, the half-spread wings motionless as an ornament. I placed a wing against the axe shaft and put pressure on it, as if on a lever. The wing snapped in half with a noise as barely perceptible as the breaking of a wafer. I put the butterfly back where I had found it. Only then did I notice that two large beetles, their wing cases as black as shiny tar, were scavenging among the corpses. 'Some more of your friends,' I called across to Hansi who stood relaxed and at home in the middle of the icefield.

Shortly after this I slipped, but it was no more than a few inches, and I began to check my slide almost as soon as it had started.

As soon as he drew level with them, Hansi picked the beetles from among the butterflies.

Now, even though the dangers grew more apparent, a feeling of elation began to surge through me. We crossed a rubble-strewn area, the top of the long column, knowing that we would have to deal with the flume, but confident that the attempt was going our way. Even the air was more pure, sharper, and I daydreamed that no one had ever breathed such air before. We'll do it!' I said, 'we'll do it,' and I repeated the phrase over and over again, like a charm.

Ice was piled at the base of the flume, but the sun was direct on it and water had begun to spout from it and cascade down the east side of the column. The flume walls were crammed with greenish ice, and all the time we could hear water running, dripping, gurgling through invisible channels. All around us the rock was coated with green algae.

We ate a little food and watched the slow spume of the water's fall towards the valley. Hansi said nothing, his face showing neither apprehension nor resolve.

'We could try the sides,' I suggested.

'Look at them,' he said.

The limestone was raw, and fell off in scales when knocked by my axe. 'Not a chance,' I agreed with reluctance. Water must have percolated through the rock just below the surface, and made the whole area unstable.

Hansi finished eating from his can and idly tossed it out into the void. 'We'll have to treat it like a chimney. You start, and I'll take over when you've had enough.'

I began to hack out stances in the lower sections of the flume, and to place pegs at the critical points. Sometimes the pegs could be struck into thin ice, almost immediately hitting the hard rock beneath, but often I could find no gap for them so I had to probe until I located at fissure. At other times I had to hammer in ice pegs, then test if they could hold my weight. Once, coming across a patch of bare rock, I found that the only way I could make the peg reliable was to wedge it with a second one. All the time I could hear the trickling sound of water.

'It would have been safer this morning,' I called back, my voice hollow and constricted, as Jean's had been within the glacier cave. Hansi gave a shout of agreement.

A short while later he took over from me, wriggling past with his face set and his breath misting. His crampons bit into the ice or scraped, jarringly, on rock.

Soon water began to spatter unevenly across us. I found that I was licking my lips obsessively, like an animal in a cage, and my mind shuffled a group of basic and unimaginative swear words as if their repetition would ease our plight. I could feel my confidence vanish as suddenly as it had arrived.

Hansi hit a slab of ice and it tumbled towards me, shattering as it went. I ducked to avoid the shards. Worse, however, was the freezing water that burst out from beneath it, and sprayed us so that our teeth began to chatter uncontrollably. We moved past as quickly as we could, but not before we had been drenched. By the time we were above it we were both shivering wildly, like fever victims.

Within the flume's upper reaches Hansi became fast, hemmed in by the ice. I could see rainbows quiver inside it like bubbles within a frozen pond, so I knew that light was reaching into the flume from above. Nevertheless there seemed to be no end of this eerie forest of dripping icicles until Hansi struck upwards at them with the cutting edge of his axe. Many had been thinned and hollowed, and they snapped easily and fell like fragile spears. I pressed my body to one side as they rattled and lanced past.

A ragged hole opened at the top of the flume. Blue sky could be seen through it, although across its rim water poured in on us in a freezing misty rain. There were no holds left, merely slithery, rotten ice. It took us another ten minutes before we could half-clamber, half-wriggle above the hole.

We stood, sodden and trembling, on rock that was tilted, glazed, the colour of glue. The high sun was just about to vanish behind the heights, but for a few moments everything around us was made brilliant by its light.

She would not make love in my rooms. Instead, at her insistence, an elaborate hoax was constructed.

Jean had an old friend, Elizabeth, who lived on the coast. I did not meet her, but Jean had to. They had not met for several years, and she had to be able to take back a story to Harry which would prove that she and Elizabeth had met, talked over old times, and promised to meet again.

I walked along the promenade and looked out across a glowering sea. I imagined Jean sitting in a nearby tearoom with her friend. Her kid gloves would be folded on the table, the paste jewellery of her hatpin would sparkle in the light, a foxfur would be round her neck. She would be a mixture of nervousness and bravado, of candour and discretion. It was even possible that she would be honest about me. They would eat fairy-cakes and drink tea, and Jean would smoke so much that the ashtray would fill with cigarette-ends marked with lipstick.

A spring wind drove a squall inland, and I had to sprint for shelter from the rain. I sat within the shelter and listened to the noise of water on the roof, and watched it rapidly drip from the canopy. It was twenty minutes before the sky cleared.

Back at the hotel I put a *Do Not Disturb* sign on the door. Jean sat beside the bed like a nurse alongside a patient. Her gestures were forcibly slow and collected, as if they masked a desire for speed and edginess. Behind her the french windows were streaked with rain, and outside, on the wrought-iron balcony, a pair of gulls perched. As we sat, one tilted back its head and gave a long repetitive cry.

'A friend of mine once took a hunting party into the mountains,' I told her. 'They were English. When they heard the call of a roe deer, they mistook it for the sound of gulls. They couldn't understand what gulls would be doing so many miles from the sea.'

'Ernest, you talk about Hansi all the time to me. Did you realise that?'

I was genuinely surprised. 'No,' I said, 'I didn't.'

We were silent for about half a minute.

'Well,' she said briskly, 'we're here. This is what we came for.' She sounded surprisingly efficient, as if she had just decided to spring-clean the room.

'Yes,' I said, not moving, 'yes.'

I did not know what she felt when, at last, we made love. Before we started she complained that my hands were cold, and I had to warm them at the sixpence-in-the-meter gas fire. After this there was an amateurish preamble with a contraceptive. But she entered into passion with a kind of planned ferocity, as if the very energy of the act would drive all other thoughts from her head.

I had expected to be more excited, less controlled. I had wanted this for a long time, and was surprised that I was neither gluttonous nor abandoned. Instead a grim satisfaction came over me, as if this very act was a confirmation of my power.

Afterwards, she cried. At first I did not know why, but when I tried to comfort her she knocked my arm aside. I had not expected her to feel guilty.

On the return journey we sat, as we had done on the outward

one, in separate compartments of the train. Harry was meeting her at the station, so I remained in the carriage until everyone else had left, and then I walked out through the barriers. Their car was pulling away from the forecourt. Jean saw me through the window and smiled stiffly, as if at a passing acquaintance. In response, I touched the brim of my hat.

I thought that our affair might end with that brief moment of adultery. Her curiosity had been satisfied, and it was even possible that her desire had been quenched. But several weeks later, after German lessons which never betrayed the fact that we had become lovers, she became more daring.

We would visit the Lake District for a couple of days, she said; I knew the area well, so I would know where we should stay. It could be a study weekend – I could read her Wordsworth and Coleridge and we would walk to the places which had inspired the poetry. We could visit the cottages where they had lived. At night, we could lie together and make love.

I asked about Harry. Surely she could not camouflage such a weekend? But Harry was going to London on a business trip, and would not be especially concerned. As far as he knew, Jean would be visiting Elizabeth again.

So our affair deepened in an old hotel by a stone bridge, with the calling of lambs from across the fields, and blossoms shaken from boughs outside our window by a warm breeze that seemed to have swept up from the very heart of Europe.

Some months later I was introduced to Harry.

Partly from boredom, and partly from curiosity, I had gone to an agricultural show. I was already daydreaming of leaving England, and it seemed appropriate that I should go to see things I might never see again. I did not expect the Swarbricks to be there.

It had rained heavily before dawn, and the grass was sodden or trampled into sludge. I had my collar turned up as I walked among the pens and stalls and tents. Animal breath steamed in the air, and everything smelled of damp – straw, wool, canvas. Across a jostle of visitors I caught sight of Jean. She was holding on to Harry's arm.

I turned abruptly to one side, pretending I had not seen her. I could tell that Harry was ingratiating himself with a group of landowners and businessmen; I could even hear his voice as it carried over the heads of the throng. Jean hung onto him like a dutiful wife.

I affected interest in a large black bull that was being tugged across a display ring by a rope. The bull's nostrils glistened with mucus and its eyes shone. The handler braced his feet, pulling tightly on the rope, and the bull moved forward with a gait that was both rolling and clumsy, as if its power had outgrown its body.

I must leave, I thought.

'Good afternoon, Mr Tinnion,' Jean said.

I was half-expecting this, and cursed myself that I had not moved further away. It did not surprise me that Jean felt compelled to introduce me to Harry. I was, she said, the teacher who had done so much to help her understand literature, and now I was teaching her German as well.

When Harry shook my hand his grip was extravagantly firm, as if he wished to register an attitude by a mere handshake.

'Ah yes,' he said with false heartiness, 'you're the romantic type, I hear.'

Only for a fraction of a second did I panic. 'I teach *the* Romantics, Mr Swarbrick. I'm sure you know that's quite a different thing.'

His jocularity was too cool, too loud. 'Of *course* I do. And German too, eh? Handy qualification, that. It's an up-and-coming country.'

Harry was a pale-faced man with a heavy jaw and large pupils to his eyes. His hair was sleek and brushed back, and he had a moustache which had been trimmed with military precision.

When Jean stood slightly apart from him she still let her hand rest on his lower arm. When she spoke her voice was lighter than normal, and her breathing more shallow. I realised she had sought me out.

'What a coincidence this is,' she said. 'I had no idea we would bump into you, Mr Tinnion.'

I smiled wanly, and wondered what she was thinking. Harry and I were strangers, yet we each knew her body intimately, as she knew ours. Perhaps this gave her a sense of excitement and danger. Perhaps, unusually, she felt privileged.

I tried to take my leave, but Harry stopped me. 'My wife tells me you're more than just a clever man, Mr Tinnion. She says you're something of an adventurer, too.'

'Mrs Swarbrick is too complimentary,' I murmured.

'Oh, I don't think so. Listen, we often have friends to dinner. Perhaps you would do us the honour sometimes?'

I avoided Jean's eyes. 'That's very kind of you.'

'I'm sure you would have a lot to tell us.'

I smiled, and tried to leave again, but he repeated his invitation before he let me go.

I did not expect to hear any further from him, and I had no desire to join the Swarbricks for a meal. When I walked out of the showground I thought I would never see him again.

But a few days later a formal invitation arrived. The card was over-elaborate, with a scalloped edge. I sat with it in my hands and wondered what to do. But there was no way out; I had to go.

The meal was unpleasant. The food was good, although not as good as I had expected. Unnecessary candles burned, and there was an ostentatious display of silverware, but I had not drunk such good wine for a long time. Each course was punctuated by cigarettes, and the evening finished with Havana cigars. I refused the cigarettes but allowed myself to be pressed into smoking a cigar. I found it acrid, but did not have the courage to stub it out. Instead, I pretended to relish its harshness.

In addition to the Swarbricks there were two other couples. One of the women had been Jean's companion when she first came to my lessons. It seemed a long time ago, although it had been less than a year.

I had little in common with any of them, and amused myself by recalling how Jean looked when she was naked, so that I sat there with an odd smile on my lips. Their conversation was a mixture of local scandal and business dealings intermixed with fragments from national politics or European problems. One had it on good authority, which she would not disclose, that the King had spoken of Mrs Simpson as his future wife; another seemed determined to elbow the discussion into dealing with Hitler and the Rhineland. I began to feel uneasy.

'Of course,' Harry said with transparent irony, 'our guest here is a much-travelled man – aren't you, Mr Tinnion? Why, you must think of us all as mere provincials. You can tell us all about what's going on in Europe.'

I wondered if he had invited me just to put me in my place. Certainly this small group was a concentration of local power and influence, and there was much talk of contacts and friends in government, politics, trade.

'I don't think of you like that,' I said, 'and I don't know what's going to happen.'

'No one's asking you to prophesy, young man,' another insisted. 'But if you're so well-travelled, you must have a good idea of what's *likely* to happen. Spain, now – what about Spain?'

'I only travel to Switzerland. I know nothing about Franco.'

'Germany?'

'I don't know Germany too well.'

'But you climb with Germans, don't you? And Austrians?'

'Look,' I said, 'I live in a small world.' I said it to appease them, for I was sure my world was much broader than theirs. 'I can only afford to go to the continent once a year – twice if I'm lucky.'

'The education board must pay you well.'

'Not really. I have to teach privately. If I worked in one of the German élite schools, I'd be much better paid.'

It was the wrong thing to say. 'You'd work in one of those?' Harry asked.

'Of course I wouldn't,' I said.

They looked at me as if they were all disappointed by what I had said.

I was suddenly angry at the injustice of all this. 'My family used to have money too, you know,' I said. 'They were just like you are now. My father invested all his money in the timber business. He lost everything.'

None of them said anything.

'I have my own opinions about Germany,' I said. 'I don't think you'd agree with them.'

'You don't agree that the country has got back onto its feet?' Harry asked. 'Surely that's a matter of fact, not opinion.'

I did not have the heart to argue. 'If you want an informed opinion,' I said, 'you should look for another expert. One that would tell you the kind of things you want to hear.'

Jean spoke with a smooth, defusing irony. 'Mr Tinnion, I hope you don't feel offended by us. I think we all may be a little bit jealous of you – after all, compared to us, you lead such an exciting life. I'm sure that you've done things that no one round this table knows anything about.'

I could not exactly say how, but I detected a hint of threat in Jean's voice. I dropped my eyes and said nothing else.

'After all,' she said, 'in a few weeks' time we'll still be here, but as for you – who knows where you'll be?'

We were suspended from pitons hammered into the rock and then bent upwards to give a better hold. I dozed fitfully, for there was no comfort in the makeshift hammock, and a distant, odd, tingling sensation troubled me. During the night I struggled out of my gloves, found a handful of frozen snow, and rubbed my fingers repeatedly with it.

As soon as I slept I was tormented by lurid dreams which jerked me awake. After a while I became blindingly thirsty. Three or four times I had to search for a drink in my rucksack, itself suspended over nothingness. I drank all the liquid without meaning to. Then, stricken by cold, I balanced precariously on naked rock and urinated out into the blackness. I thought of being naked with Jean, our bodies warm as hot bread, the sheets freshly laundered. My imagination flared vividly, but I could do nothing but lie there, trussed up, waiting for the dawn.

Just before first light we disentangled ourselves from our perch and made ready for the day. A delicate fine mist clung to the wall, and the sun was distant and watery when it rose. The lines of the mountain were softened, as if seen through gauze.

Hansi held the altimeter in his hand. I was already dreading what I could be told.

'It's up,' he said.

'How much?'

'Sixty metres.'

For more than a minute neither of us spoke. Instead we looked around the precipices and upwards and out at the sky. Behind the thin greyness we could see blue.

'It's possible that the reading is false,' he said after a while.

'But you don't believe that.'

'No.'

'And therefore?'

'We don't want to be caught by a storm while we're here. Our chances are better higher up. If we can get into the lee of one of the rock spines at the side of the web, there's a chance of shelter.'

'Hansi, once we're on the web, we're completely exposed.'

'You want to retreat, Ernest?'

'It's a matter of prudence. Surely we'll be better off further down.'

76

'We gain nothing by running scared, like frightened little boys.'

'Except our lives?'

He smiled. 'You forget I was involved in a retreat from the Eiger.'

I did not answer.

'We're wasting time,' he said. 'Let's go.'

There was no further discussion, and we moved up the next section as quickly as we could. For about half an hour conditions remained the same. The sun did not disperse the mist and, if anything, the mountain became softer and less substantial, like something gradually dissolving.

We stopped for a late, hasty breakfast. Before we ate, Hansi took a handful of snow and rubbed his fingers to increase circulation. I noticed that the bruising on them had deepened. Even though our eyes met, he said nothing.

Later in the morning the mist began to thicken noticeably. Strands of it could be seen, wound like ghostly streamers around pinnacles. The light became dimmer and more diffuse, so that it was not like morning light at all. Before long everything darkened into a thick cloud which closed tightly around us, carrying within it flurries of snow.

We were on a perpendicular cliff of stratified black rock, each band of it as high as the wall of a room. There were plenty of good holds, but these rapidly began to fill with snow. We had to climb with bare hands, and the snow melted under the warmth of our fingertips and then froze again. Soon each hold had to be cleared before we could use it. The greyness curdled, obscuring everything, and a low moaning sound began to be heard from every side as snow began to pour down even more heavily. It cascaded down the rock in runnels. Looking up I could see it form from nothing, as in some alchemical trick, and swarm at us in huge blinding flakes. I could smell its eerie purity and taste its razor-sharp iciness on my lips. By the time we reached the top of the pitch its rock basins were overflowing in tiny avalanches.

A few more steps and we were on top of a spur of rock with a spume of snow streaming from it. I shook my head at Hansi, but he seized the shoulder of my coat and said, 'We must go on. It's the only safe thing to do.'

A terrible doubt grasped me, and suddenly I was not sure where we were. 'This is the web, isn't it?' I asked, my voice cracking. I felt I could be living in a dream, and that what stood in front of me was not Hansi, but something disguised as him.

'If we can do this,' he urged, 'the Versücherin is solved. Forever.'

We had climbed the rock, but now we had to buckle on crampons for the ice. My fingers were numb. I fumbled and dropped the left one. It clinked on the rock, then slid a few inches and lodged on the very edge of the cliff we had just scaled. Quickly I retrieved it and, shaking, fastened it to my boot. Hansi was staring at me. His jacket creases were full of snow.

'This is madness,' I said.

'What would you have us do, Ernest? Stay here and freeze to death?'

We stepped onto the web.

At first I thought it was uniform, but as we kicked and hacked our way upwards I discovered that, almost imperceptibly, the ice dipped and swelled. It seemed that its own mass was making it slide downwards with glacial slowness, for we passed across a series of shallow waves. At first I led, and, as we struggled, runnels of fresh snow began to spill and trickle across the gloomy surface.

After an indeterminate length of time we heard the hissing grumble of a larger fall, somewhere over to our left and hidden by cloud. I knew that we were as exposed as a target, so I hammered in an ice peg and waited for a cataract to come grinding out of the darkness and shake us from our holds.

Nothing happened.

I looked back at Hansi. I was shocked to see his face encrusted with snow; then I realised that my own, too, must be like this. He shouted something at me which I could not hear, and only when he repeated it did I understand. He was saying that we must secure ourselves at every metre.

So we clawed our way forward, fixing ourselves on chilling, grainy ice that had become the colour of smoke, whilst all around us the wall howled. I became increasingly weary. I tried to persuade myself that this storm must end sometime, but it showed no sign of doing so. I ceased to think logically, but continued to cut at the surface as, once again, I repeated a phrase slavishly, over and over. We were going for the summit, we were going for the summit.

I was marooned on the web. Hansi tugged at the rope to make me stop, and I hung there while he slowly inched his way past me to take the lead. Afterwards I began to follow him, still working automatically.

Fragments of rock came cartwheeling all around me. I gazed at them and wondered why they were falling. Then, more by instinct that anything else, I dug in with the ice axe and hoped desperately that Hansi was secure at the head of the rope. The air began to fill with a rushing, grating, slithering noise, and snow started to pour thickly across me. It cut out light and air. I buried my face next to the ice and tried to draw a last deep breath, but the cascade had drawn the air with it. I gasped like a drowning man, my lungs full of freezing splinters. The avalanche rocked and mauled me, and I could feel my hands begin to slip on the axe haft. Even if I could hold on, I was convinced that a force such as this would spring the blade away from its hold, sweeping me with it down the wall. The snow began to pack underneath me, forcing me out from the ice layer by layer. I began to think that I was part of some absurd mathematical demonstration, and that more and more pressure would be applied until breaking point was reached and I was plucked helplessly from the web.

Then, suddenly, the pressure decreased. I gasped convulsively, although I could not open my eyes. Then the avalanche began again.

There was the same buffeting, the same lack of air, the same leverage on my body. This time the fall was short, but I could still feel my grip gradually slide down the slippery wood of the axe, and above me the rope vibrated as if in time to some great mysterious engine.

The avalanche petered out in a scuttering rush of grains. I found that my lip was frozen to the ice. I pulled my head away sharply, and felt nothing when the skin tore even though a few bright drops of blood fell on the snow. By the time I had raised my head further the bleeding had already stopped.

I peered at Hansi, who I could see through a swirl of mist and blown snow. He waved his hand feebly, like a man exhausted.

I laboured up to him, and he peered at me through a cracked mask of a face.

'You're cut,' he said.

I shook my head. 'You did well to hang on. I didn't think we were going to get out.'

'Ernst, snow will be building up within the exit gullies. If a balcony is formed, then breaks away, we'll have to endure the same thing again.'

We stood braced on the angle, breathing heavily, with the snow freezing.

'We have to get out of here,' Hansi said, patiently and without drama.

A tremor passed through me that was so fierce I had to grip more tightly.

'We must go up,' he said with calm simplicity.

I shook my head again. 'Hansi, I can't. I've had enough.' I had not intended to say this, but once spoken it seemed that I should have said it hours, days ago. I had allowed myself to be carried away by the dream of transcendence and fame. I had no need, no right, to be on this mountain.

Hansi moved a step further up the face.

'I mean it,' I said vehemently.

'Ernst, we cannot go back. You know that as well as I do.'

'I don't care about the mountain, Hansi, I don't care about anything or anybody. I just want to get off this wall. I don't want to be the first man up, I don't want a triumph, I don't want to be immortalised by Max Volkwein. I want to live. If that means failure, then I'll take failure.'

'You were at the bottom of the rope just now. That means that, for the moment, you may be stronger than me. Ernst, you lead for a few metres. Then I'll take over again.'

I stared grimly at him, refusing to move.

'Ernst,' he explained, 'I have stopped planning for success. Now I am planning only for our survival.'

Time seeped away from us. There was only the sheerness of the ice, the dark pressure of cloud, the scatterings and blasts of snow, the slither of cascades from invisible heights.

'I'll lead,' I said.

We moved upwards, the ropes stiffening in the cold, our breathing harsh. I had to concentrate on each haul, each awkward, troubling step. I wished that I could be somewhere else where I could wear different clothes, where there would be sunshine and laughter and a band playing in the distance. I could be lounging among thick, rich clover. But all I was doing was working, methodically but infinitely slowly, wrestling each extra foothold from the web.

The snow began to harden and turn to hail, which rattled furiously and stung my cheeks. Everything became blacker, as if we had misjudged the day and the sun had set.

I leaned into the surface, my lobsterclaws bored into it. I fixed a piton and pushed the rope through its linked ring. Around me was an undifferentiated greyness from which broad swaths of hail were hurled.

Then an odd change made itself heard – a variation, a new

pattern. I registered it, but did not know what it was. A kind of rolling swish formed somewhere above me, and a few stray pieces of crusted ice plunged past without touching me. I was slow-witted and cold and did not know what was happening.

Then I realised, and tried to burrow into the ice at the same time as I tried to haul my rucksack over my head.

The avalanche hit me gently at first, as if a giant snowman, somehow come alive, cuffed me jokingly about head and shoulders. But then I was struck with increasing weight and violence, and the snow stuffed itself down my collar and up my sleeves. I breathed it in; it cemented around my eyes, thrust itself into my nostrils, pushed itself into my ears so that I became deaf to its feathery roar. A pain grew rapidly in my arms and chest, and I thought that it would become intolerable very soon.

But, instead, everything became dreamily unreal. I did not know if I was still hanging to my fixed point or floating away from it, unharmed, into a world with neither gravity nor frost. I thought that I was still lashed to my end of the rope, but that the rope was lighter than a ribbon although strong as a hawser. I floated easily, as if in a salt-rich sea, and knew that another person, perhaps Hansi, anchored the ribbon with a grip that was secure, perfect, comforting.

Then, curiously, I was not floating at all, but wedged between slabs of ice, as if somehow I had fallen within a glacier. I could see nothing, but knew that I was being carried along with slow, limitless force.

There was the sound in my ears like the tunnelling of moles and, as if from far away, the noise of hail returned. Pallor and darkness flickered around me like polar lights. Something cold and wooden jabbed at my eyes, nostrils, ears, then forced themselves into my mouth until I retched.

I opened my eyes and saw that wide plates of hail were scattered across the icefield like giant scabs. Near by a rope, dripping with icicles, was coiled. Someone whom I did not at first recognise was prodding at my face with bare hands.

'Ernst,' he said to me, 'Ernst.' I was shaken and my face was slapped.

I looked at Hansi. He brought his face close to mine.

'Well done,' he said, speaking carefully, 'you hung on. But we are pinned to the web like victims. We must get off.'

I was puzzled. I was certain this had happened before, and that we were condemned to repeat our period of trial, time after time.

'You must hold on,' Hansi continued; 'we can make it to the nearest spur if you don't give in.'

He vanished from sight, but I could hear him cut a stance for me just at my feet, and within a few seconds he had eased my boots into it. The hail around me thinned for a few seconds, then returned with all its former ferocity.

Hansi came back beside me and unshouldered his pack, loosing crescents of hail as he did. He hung it on to a secondary peg then began to force the straps through the buckles. I noticed that his hands were still bare. When he opened the top flap he had to lever it, for it was as stiff as board.

He found the schnapps and withdrew it. Unscrewing the top was a different matter, and as soon as it was loose he dropped it so that it vanished.

Our eyes met. 'To hell with it,' he said, and passed it to me.

'I can't hold it. Not just yet.'

He poured some into my mouth then took a swig himself. The liquid burned my tongue then passed down my gullet in a slow scorch. I could smell berries. 'We shouldn't drink too much,' I warned him.

'We can't keep it now,' he responded. 'There's nothing broken, I don't think. You seem to be coming to.' His face split in a crazy smile. 'We'll do it,' he said, 'don't you worry.'

He offered me more schnapps. I shook my head. 'It could make us haemorrhage.' It was true: the blood vessels, made fragile by the cold, could rupture under the effect of alcohol.

'One more,' he said. We took a drink each and then he tossed the bottle to one side. Ironically, it fell only a few feet away and immediately lodged in a patch of freezing hail. I wanted to kick it free, but I could not reach.

'I'm tired,' I said.

'You mustn't sleep. Ernst. You can't.'

I gazed at Hansi. He looked more weary than I had ever seen him, and his face was lined like an old man's. There was a sallow tinge around his eyes.

'Where are your gloves?' I asked.

'I had to take them off. Their fingers were too clumsy. I had to clear your mouth and nostrils of snow, otherwise you could have choked.'

I nodded, as if satisfied by a schoolboy's excuse. 'Where are they, then?'

'Gone. I must have forgotten to secure them. They must be hundreds of feet below us by now.'

I tried to smile at him but could not. 'You forgot a basic rule,' I said.

He nodded. 'There are other pairs in the rucksack, but they must be at the bottom. I daren't risk searching too deeply.' He brought himself nearer to me. 'I've lost one of the ropes. I didn't know if you were alive or dead, so I had to secure myself to one and come up on it. I don't have the strength to retrieve it, so I've cut myself free. But it's all right, we have rope enough to get us to the nearer crag. It'll be shelter for the night.'

The hail lessened, and began to turn to snow. Just above us the cloud must have opened, for a shapeless patch of sunlight shone momentarily on the ice before dimming again.

'Hansi, are we almost at the top?'

'Yes. We must be.'

It was only a short distance to the crag, but it seemed as if we would never make it. Hansi led as if each step were a matter of life and death. Behind him I was confused, listless, and uncoordinated. When I finally got to the crag I was hit by a form of shock. I began to tremble, and wanted to vomit, but all I suffered was a painful series of retching spasms.

We treated the crag as a target, as an end in itself. Now that we had reached it, our plight seemed even more desperate and more hopeless. I looked up at the rock, which was black, hideously broken, and wedged with sections of ice.

'Your gloves,' I said to Hansi, 'you must find another pair.'

'Yes,' he said, 'yes.'

But as I watched he took hold of a piece of rock the size of a brick, which he pulled effortlessly from the crag wall. He placed it on the ice at our feet. It grated for an inch or so, then tobogganed out of sight.

The sun came through again, and for half a minute or so the ice glittered before the snow closed around us once more.

5

HANSI AND MAX CAME BACK THE FOLLOWING MORNING. JEAN AND I were eating breakfast, and we had been joined by Bruno. I did my best to be pleasant to the boy, but his self-absorption unsettled me. After a while, perhaps thinking that it was one thing which we had in common, he began to talk about the bodies in the church. Apparently he saw nothing bizarre in talking about the processes of natural mummification while we ate. I cast a despairing glance at Jean, but she responded by raising her eyebrows in an attitude of amused challenge. When she had returned to me the night before, she had tried to explain the boy's character. 'He's quite immature,' she had said, 'but probably a lot more clever than most children his age. I understand him, I think. He's been through a lot – losing his mother *and* his father must have been terrible – so his interests have become too focused, too intense. Go easy on him, Ernest. Once you get to know him, he's really nice.'

But, as Clara served more food to Bruno, it was difficult to tolerate him. 'Of course,' he insisted with a certain grim thoroughness, 'you need a desiccating agent. Extremes of temperature often do it, because then the agents of decay cannot work. So a dry, desert heat, or an intense dry cold will both do the trick.'

I saw Jean suppress a smirk at my expense. He would grow out of this period, she had said; he would change. But I did not see Bruno as being on the brink of development. Instead I saw him as becoming more isolated and obsessed. Unless something dramatic changed his life, I saw his adult self already established in the way he spoke now.

After a few minutes Otto came to our table. He leaned across it and, in a stage whisper I was sure could be overheard by the other guests, he told me that there were two people approaching the pension. 'It seems they have come a long way,' he added with over-heavy significance.

I nodded, and tried to appear indifferent.

'Will it be Uncle?' Bruno asked, and for the first time I heard affection within his voice.

'I think so,' I said.

Jean reached over and squeezed his hand. 'It must be,' she said, 'otherwise Herr Seematter wouldn't have mentioned it.'

It took Hansi and Max another half hour to reach us. By this time the other guests had left, and we could sit in the room by ourselves. Clara made more food in readiness, and I could smell coffee boiling in the kitchen.

Bruno ran out to meet them, but Jean and I remained seated. When they came into the Seematters' I thought that they both looked tired, even though they were smiling. Bruno had his hands round Max's arm.

They sat down and we all shook hands as if in a ritual. I was cool towards them. Perhaps detecting this, they surprised me by first of all asking Jean how she had enjoyed her trip to the glacier. Hansi, in particular, seemed too eager to be solicitious and worthy, as if he was trying to make amends.

'Tell me about the summit,' I said after a minute or so of this.

I noticed Max give a small private smile, almost like a grimace. I could not understand why he had done it.

'The east ridge is easy,' Hansi said, 'and it's the perfect escape from the wall. But there is no way on to it other than going right to the top. We have to succeed or retreat.'

He looked round at us all, relishing his command.

'At its lowest point,' he continued, 'the ridge is broad. Then it ascends across rock, verglas, and frozen snow towards the summit. Providing you are well protected, and fit, the climb is not demanding. Isn't that right, Max?'

Max nodded. I felt a twinge of jealousy at their closeness and common purpose.

'That's true,' Otto butted in quickly, eager to remind us once again that he knew the east ridge.

Hansi continued. 'The summit is a high, tilted plateau. It is bare, polished ice, apart from the cairn. There is a log book buried within it. We opened the book. There are fine names in there – the best.'

He looked closely at me. His eyes were proud and, I thought, a little scared. I knew that he had found Toni Kurz's name there.

'I made Hansi sign it,' Max said, 'because I wanted to write my own name as well.'

Otto interrupted once again. 'The next time, the climbers will be able to write *north wall* after their names.'

'The plateau slopes away towards the north face,' Hansi said, 'and it becomes very steep. It does not fall very far – a few hundred metres, no more – and at its base there are the stumps of rock that come up out of the ice web. You can see them if you descend for only a short distance.'

'We would come up through one of those?' I asked.

Hansi nodded. 'We were late at the summit, so we could not stay as long as we would have liked. We buried the stores within the cairn and set off down the ridge. The sun was already sinking and it had become bitterly cold. Otto had told us about the old hut, and we made for that.'

Quite suddenly he shuddered. Max looked at him with the air of a curious professor.

'It was a terrible night,' Hansi explained. 'The hut was infested by mice. They kept us awake by running across us, even across our faces. We got so angry that we started to throw things at them, but each time we did they darted out of the way. We must have looked like people in a comedy film, but at the time it was difficult to see the joke. It seemed so ironic, so unjust – I was full of confidence, and it was absurd to have mice scurrying across us.'

'It must have been horrible,' Jean said. 'I couldn't have done it. As far as I was concerned, it wouldn't be worth it.'

'It's worth anything and everything,' Hansi said excitedly. 'Ernest, I feel good about this climb. Everything is in our favour.'

'And the Italians?' I asked. 'Is that why the two of you went, so that we could save time in case the Italians came?'

Hansi seemed surprised that I should ask. 'Of course,' he said.

'*Are* there any Italians?'

Hansi, puzzled, looked at Max, then back at me. 'Max believes that there might be. Very soon.'

'You can't know that,' I challenged Max.

He smiled at me. There was a patronising curl to one lip. 'But I can,' he said.

'You suspect, that's all,' I said.

'You forget,' Max said, 'that I have been an observer of competitions and races for many years. It is my job; I am just as much of a reporter as a man who writes down words, perhaps more so. I know how the pressure builds, how the fever takes hold. You and Hansi are a special kind of man, Ernst. But there are others just like you.'

'This shouldn't be a race,' Jean protested. 'You make everything more dangerous if you rush at things like that.'

'But Jean,' Hansi said, 'that's the whole point.'

'*I* thought the whole point was to get to the top,' she said. 'You've all talked about planning and weighing things up and only going if you're certain. Now you want to scramble for it like children playing king-of-the-castle.'

'Jean,' Hansi said, 'if we hesitate, someone will be on the top before us. Everything will be wasted if that happens.'

Unexpectedly she turned to Max. 'What do *you* think of all this?' she demanded.

His gaze was cool, his reply measured. 'I do not think you appreciate its significance, Mrs Tinnion. I understand that in England you are poor, and without much national confidence or political direction. Across much of Europe, however, there is a revival of pride. Everything is being made new. And people believe that things once thought impossible are now within their grasp. Climbers are ready to attack sheer walls with intelligence, courage, and the force of will. No longer do they use the old methods. Now it is necessary to be fast, light, well-equipped, or else the walls will defeat them. I could quote you, if you wish, the names of climbers and mountains. Otto will bear me out.'

'You're not answering me,' she said.

'You've seen my photographs. That is how I make my living. My speciality is human endeavour; I photograph those in the vanguard. It is a good job, and it pays me well.'

'You speak as if you have no part to play, but that's not true.'

He smiled disarmingly at her.

'You've just helped the attempt by placing stores on the summit,' she went on. 'You're not just a bystander. You don't just record.'

'You wouldn't deny me my own small part in the making of history?'

'Max, your work doesn't just show success and glory. You're just as likely, and perhaps just as keen, to photograph pain and humiliation.'

'Sometimes I have unpleasant duties, yes. But I will do what I can to make sure that Hansi and your husband will be first to the top of that mountain by the north face.'

She nodded. 'Of course. You don't have their obsession, do you? You can't fully share in this madness that they have.'

Hansi and I exchanged glances. He shrugged as if Jean's comments were unimportant.

Max, meanwhile, had begun to grin broadly, as if Jean had

discovered a secret he had only half-hidden from her. 'I am nothing but a dilettante,' he said, self-mockingly.

'You don't think of yourself like that. I imagine that you believe you have a broader perspective, and a better understanding of events, than any of us.'

'*Everyone* believes that of themselves, Jean. You are saying nothing new.'

'Perhaps you have better cause than most to believe it of yourself.'

Max spread his hands as if he would not contest such an assertion.

I was watching Jean carefully. She had spoken with such control and ease that I was surprised to see her suddenly bite her lower lip, as if a nervous spasm had passed through her. I almost reached out a hand to touch her, but did not.

'Max,' she asked, 'what would you advise me to do?'

'Jean, it is not up to me –'

'Please.'

Max looked at me and I looked down at the table. Otto had walked away, rather deliberately, to consult his shelf of scrapbooks, whilst Hansi was peering into the bottom of a glass as if there was something to be found there.

'It is a woman's duty to stand by her husband,' he said at last. There was a slight inflection on the last word, as if he had hesitated before choosing it.

'Why?' she demanded.

'Because of the legal and moral bonds that tie them together. There can be no other answer.'

I thought of Bruno's mother, making her escape into another life, leaving only her son behind her.

'I don't accept that,' Jean said. 'There's a higher law than that. There must be. If a man is about to sacrifice himself because of some crazy scheme, it's his wife's duty to try and prevent it. It's *anyone*'s duty to do that.'

'There are higher laws, yes. But not the kind that you talk about. There are laws of destiny and necessity. Your husband, and Hansi, are obeying those laws. You should not deflect them from their purpose.'

She shook her head as if she could not accept such a proposition.

Hansi, who had begun to rub one hand inside the other, cleared his throat in a pointed manner.

'Ernst,' he said, 'we must make arrangements to leave immediately.'

I looked at him disbelievingly. I had refused to consider that our departure would be so imminent.

'We cannot, must not delay any further,' he continued. 'The Italians could be marching towards the wall even as we speak.'

'We can't start now,' I protested.

'You said you would be ready.'

'I *am*.'

'Well then, we must leave. We'll take our equipment to the farm buildings, rest there, and begin before dawn. That way we will be already high on the face when the sun comes up.' He stood up, pushing back the heavy chair as he did. 'Come,' he said, 'it is time to say goodbye to our friends.'

I got to my feet slightly dazed. Jean was staring at the far wall as if she did not wish to look at me.

'I'll help you as far as the farm,' Max said. When Hansi began to protest he held out a hand. 'No, I'm not tired. And I shall sleep better than you for the next few nights.'

Bruno asked if he could come, but Max told him he could not. When the boy looked disappointed Max hugged him round the shoulders and told him that, before long, he would be able to climb mountains, not just watch men depart for them.

'A photograph,' Otto said, 'I must take a photograph.'

We went outside. I tried not to look up at the Versücherin although I could see that Hansi was gazing at it as if at an apparition. I glanced across at Jean. She had a reproachful, hurt expression on her face which hardened into determination as soon as she saw me look at her.

'Please,' Otto said, clasping a box camera in his hands, 'let me take you against the mountain.' Despite the agility of his fingers, he seemed clumsy with the camera, and juggled it as if he did not quite understand how to work it. I realised that he felt intimidated by the presence of Max, and that he was covering up as well as he could. Behind him Clara appeared, rubbing her hands on an apron.

Otto intended to take several shots of us, and decided that the best place for us to stand would be on a low bank at the far side of the road. If we stood on top of it he could stand in the road and frame both ourselves and the north wall. The sun was already high over the mountain, and the slope of the bank was in shadow. I could see Max weighing up the tonal values of such an arrangement, but he said nothing.

'Please,' Otto said, 'all four of you.'

Max stepped back and waved his hand to indicate a refusal. Like many photographers, he was obviously unhappy about his own photograph being taken.

We clambered up onto the bank and faced Otto. Our shadows fell towards him.

'Mrs Tinnion,' he said, 'would you stand between them?'

She obeyed and, at a further request, we put our arms round each other. I could detect Jean's resistance to my touch.

There was a click as the shutter opened and closed.

'Now, just the two of you,' Otto said, but this was followed by a grunt of exasperation. 'The film is finished,' he said.

Clara and Otto began to disagree about who had used so much of the film. Clara asked Max if he had any that he could let them have, but he shook his head and explained that he used a different size. 'Ah well,' Otto said, resigning himself, 'I shall have to let you make the record, Herr Volkwein. And this camera will be loaded ready for your successful return, gentlemen.'

Hansi left us to check that his motorcycle was still secure in the barn. Max accompanied him, while Otto and Clara went back into the pension.

'Well?' Jean asked.

'What?'

'Give it up, Ernest. You still have time.'

'I can't.'

'Do I have to ask you again? Would it help if I went on my knees to you? I'll do that, if you insist.'

I shook my head. 'There's no point.' And suddenly I was filled with anger. 'This was always going to happen, you know. I always was going to climb the north wall.'

'Ernest, I didn't realise how dangerous it would be. And now that you have me, your life has changed. You're responsible for me now.'

'I have to go. Even if it's only to keep peace with myself.'

'You have to go because Hansi is more important to you than I am, and what he says, what he does, is more important that what I say or do.'

'That's not true.' I made a gesture of exasperation. 'Jean, you went along with the arrangement knowing exactly what it was.'

'Yes,' she said, 'and I believed that our love would change everything. But you're not willing to let it do that, are you, Ernest? I have given up my whole life for you, and thrown away a husband, security, friends. I've destroyed my reputation, given up the chance of independence, and it has all been for you. What have you given up?'

I did not reply.

'Nothing,' she said; 'that's what you've given up, nothing.'

She turned and began to walk back to the pension. I ran after her and tried to catch her arm, but she twisted it away. 'Get off me,' she said in a choked voice, and hurried on.

94

In the few seconds that her face had been turned to me I saw that it was streaked by tears.

I stood in the middle of the road, alone, with the sun casting my shadow in front of me. A few yards away I saw Max at the barn door. He was the only one who could have seen our argument, and as I looked at him, he turned away and stepped inside.

The farm was built of rough, irregularly shaped stone. Many of the slates on the roof had become dislodged and slipped downwards. Lines of white paint had been traced around the door, converging above it in a rough cross. Two tiny windows, each also crowned with a faint cross, were set in the walls, and there was a heavy wooden door which stood ajar.

The door was open wide enough for us to walk through without pushing it further, but Hansi moved it another few inches. We stood within an empty byre. Cracked limewash hung from the walls in dirty flakes and the floor was caked with dry, crumbling cow-dung.

'I hope it's not all through the building,' I said, only half-jokingly.

Hansi did not answer me, but walked across the floor and paused at a second door. Max entered the byre, shouldering his pack higher, and squinted round as if judging the light.

We went through the second doorway, and Hansi stopped us at the threshold. Here was what must have been the family room. Inside were two roughly carved bedframes, each too heavy to move. Otherwise there were just bare walls, a ceiling thick with cobwebs, and an old broken stool. But there was a heap of ash still in the hearth, and broken planking was stacked beside it as if to feed a fire. Dust coated every ledge, but it had been swept from one bedrame, and the open floor in front of us was marked with boots.

Hansi walked across the floor to a third door, which must have led to a dairy, for I saw within the room a bench hollowed as if to hold pails. He peered inside, then turned back to us. 'No one,' he said. His voice echoed hollowly, as if he had spoken the first words in a haunted room.

'Who would be here?' I asked.

'A tramp?' he suggested.

Max came into the room, heaved his pack from his back and set it on the bedframe. 'There's only one,' he said. 'If there had been two, the other bed would have been cleaned.'

'It's not a comfortable place,' I said.

'It'll be more comfortable than our nights on the mountain,' Hansi replied. 'There's even a spring behind the building.' He crouched by the hearth. 'There's still warmth in these ashes,' he said. Then he found that a metal hook, fixed into the wall, could still be rotated outwards. 'Someone stayed overnight,' he continued, 'they have heated water on this.'

'It must be a tramp,' I suggested again.

Hansi stood up and dashed his hands free of ash. 'It's someone who will be scouting the wall even as we speak, Ernst. We did well to set off when we did. The rest of them will be here in a day or so.'

We remade the fire while Max prowled round the building. We made use of the planking and other slivers of wood which we found within the dairy. Before long the fire was throwing out substantial heat. Clara had lent us an old kettle which Max would take back to her, and soon we had it filled with water and hung over the fire. Hansi, like a diligent housewife, swept the beds and the floor as if he was trying to rid the farm of all traces of its other occupant.

Every five minutes or so we went outside and scanned what we could see of the north wall.

We sat outside to drink our tea, and Max took our photographs. Then we restowed our equipment into two packs ready for the climb.

Max was restless, and behaved as if everything had to be observed, noted, recorded. After a while he walked to the top of the nearest rise and looked down on us through his viewfinder. When he returned he told us to expect a visitor.

We both looked at him and he stared back at us with a laconic smile.

'Just one?' Hansi asked.

'That's all. I suspect he's been testing the lower part of the face. If he set off this morning, he could even have been as far as Friendly Ledge before he turned back.'

'How long will it be before he's here?'

'Not long. Forty minutes or so.'

'Did he see you?'

'Probably. Anyway, he would have seen that.'

He pointed to the smoke which came from the chimney.

'We have announced our presence,' Hansi said.

'And your purpose,' Max added.

We sat outside and waited for the climber. While we waited we hardly spoke. High up among the precipices a raven called.

The man came down the slopes with a purposeful but calm gait. As he approached we could see that he was wearing a red shirt, braces, and corduroy trousers that were cut off just below the knees. 'An Italian,' Hansi murmured.

The man was dark-haired, in his thirties, and had a tanned, narrow face. As he approached us he raised a hand in greeting. Max moved to one side, his camera raised like a shield.

'It's him,' Hansi said as the man walked rapidly towards us. We got to our feet. 'Signor Bissolati,' Hansi said, without even the trace of a query in his voice.

The response was in heavily accented German. 'Herr Kirchner, it is an honour to meet you again.'

Hansi made the introductions, we shook hands, and then Bissolati sat with us and drank tea which Hansi offered him from his own mug.

For a short while we held a strained conversation about the likelihood of the weather lasting, and about Bissolati's climbing boots which, he said, were many years old and which he was sure would last until the end of his climbing days.

'You are surveying our wall,' Hansi said suddenly. He spoke in a mild tone with a hint of reproof.

'*Your* wall, gentlemen?'

Hansi nodded to reinforce his claim to possession. 'Of course. There is no point in disguising our intentions – you will have recognised them already. We, in turn, have recognised yours.'

Bissolati's expression did not alter.

'We shall begin our climb in just a few hours,' Hansi went on.

Bissolati nodded slightly, as if digesting new information.

'You are a famous climber,' Hansi said. 'There are plenty of other faces on which you can test your skill and your fame. We want this to be ours. No one else's.'

'And I, of course, was certain that it would belong to me, and to my team. None of us owns anything, Herr Kirchner.'

Hansi remained impassive.

Bissolati looked around us. 'You have all heard of me – yes? Well, you know, then, that I have never been first on anything. Across the backbone of Europe the severe walls have all come under attack – the Matterhorn north, the Dru, the Cima Grande, the Eiger, the Piz Badile. We have men like the Schmidt brothers, Allain and Leininger, Cassin, Molteni, Valsecchi –' And he extended a hand towards Hansi. 'Kirchner,' he added. 'Friends, I have never been first on such climbs, or among such company. I am like you – just like you. I need to be first.'

Hansi did not respond. Max looked carefully at us all.

'I am growing old,' Bissolati continued. 'I am thirty-four, which is older than any of you. And before long, none of us will be able to make journeys such as this.'

'You have many years left in you,' I said, in a conciliatory way.

He turned to me. 'You misunderstand me. Or do you not realise in England that before long all Europe will be at war?'

I felt a sudden thrill of horror. His statement was so matter-of-fact that it carried all the weight of a prophecy.

Hansi smiled. 'You exaggerate. There are troubles, yes, and disagreements, but Europe is at the brink of a new age. Isn't that right, Max?'

Before Max could say anything Bissolati gave a humourless laugh, and raised his hands so that his fingers pointed to his own chest. 'Look at my own country. We are so top-heavy with munitions and troops that we *must* use them. Our people are eager for the next Abyssinia; they think it is a time of glory, the time for a new empire. Look at Spain – what has happened to the government of Spain?' He turned to Max. 'Your country is giving arms to Franco; you know that it is. And our country is sending men.'

'These things happen all the time,' Max said; 'there is nothing unusual about what is happening.'

'What do you think will go next, Herr Volkwein – Austria?'

'The Austrians must decide their own fate,' Max said. 'And all this will be achieved without more than the necessary force. Wars will be confined to unimportant, out-of-the-way places.'

'Whatever happens,' Hansi said, 'this country will want to be neutral.'

'And where would all our climbers be?' Bissolati asked. 'I shall tell you: they will be in tanks, in aeroplanes, and graves. Even I might not be old enough to escape involvement. I must take every chance as if it were my last, friends. Europe will be a dark place for many, many years.'

I could see that Hansi had been swayed by Bissolati's plea. He began to say something, then thought better of it.

'You need have no fear of us,' Bissolati continued. 'The other members of my team will not be here until tomorrow. By then you will be already high on the mountain.' He glanced at Max. 'You're a three-man rope?'

'No. Two only,' Max replied.

He shrugged. 'There should be four of you, at least. We shall be six. And we shall follow in your footsteps.'

'As Herr Kirchner says,' Max said, 'there are other north walls.'

'But only one Versücherin. As there is only one Eiger.' Bissolati turned to Hansi. 'I knew Rainer and Angerer.'

Hansi nodded.

'It was a tragedy on that wall.'

'We did what we could to get Toni.'

'Of course. You should not reproach yourselves for having failed. But do not think that I wish to attempt the Eiger – there are too many eyes on that target already. *This* mountain is the one that I want.'

'The Eiger is a large prize,' I suggested.

'The Germans will be concentrating all their best men on it. It is rumoured that the first ones to climb it will be given Olympic medals.'

'I didn't know that,' Hansi said. 'Is that true, Max?'

'That will depend on *who* is first,' he replied.

'You mean they would have to be German nationals?'

'Of course. And they would have to be acceptable –' he hesitated, then picked a word, 'socially.'

Bissolati made a dismissive, snorting noise. 'When I was a young man, I believed that climbing was an adventure of the spirit as well as the body.'

'You're right,' Max said.

'But I thought it was personal, to do with yourself alone. Now I find that it is part of a political movement. Climbers are examples, heroes; they justify training, education, beliefs. I would rather live in the days of innocence.' He paused. 'That is another reason, friends. Within a year or so, I do not know if I will be able to stomach the new breed of climber.'

He stood up, thanked us for the tea, and shook hands again.

'I wish you well with your attempt. It would be dishonest of me to wish you success. Don't forget – we shall be at your heels. The slightest weakness, a wrong decision, and we shall overtake you.'

'That won't happen,' Hansi said.

Bissolati shrugged. 'In that case, we shall have to applaud you.'

We thanked him and Hansi said, 'You *are* one of the best. The brotherhood of climbers knows this to be true.'

I saw a tiny smile cross Max's face as he heard the word *brotherhood*.

'Signor Bissolati,' Max said, 'I'll join you on the way down. We can talk over many things. These two young men need to get what sleep they can. Their great adventure will start very soon.'

We gathered Max's things together. Before he left he insisted on taking some photographs of us. We stood beside the building with our arms folded. Behind him, some way down the path, Bissolati had stopped to wait for him. He was staring up at the Versücherin wall, and he looked like a man staring his own future in the face.

6

LIGHT DRAINED AWAY. THE ICE HAD BECOME GREY AND SHINY, LIKE the colour of distant mudflats stippled with luminescence. Hansi left me safe against a protrusion on the crag and explored its lee side. Erosion had made it rich with holds and ledges, but I could see that most were unsafe and that they would crumble under pressure. Once on the sheltered side of the vertical spine, however, he found an overhang under which it was safe to rest. He had checked by jabbing at its underside with his axe.

Once we were there, he discovered that, a little further up the crag, there was a more favourable place. 'We're in luck,' he said, apparently without irony. As gloom deepened on the face we scrambled towards a narrow cave. We were too weary to obey procedure, and the rope caught in our crampons several times.

The recess was narrow, and had apparently been formed when a large part of the cliff had fallen away. We knocked loose the hard crust of snow which had almost sealed its mouth and hauled ourselves into it.

Once we were inside, the cave seemed even tinier, with a floor that shelved towards the outer lip. But it was still a better shelter than either of us could have reasonably hoped to find. Tipsy with fatigue, I thought of resting there like wounded soldiers until fellow warriors came to rescue us.

Hansi wedged me as firmly as he could against the walls. I was still shaking. Desperate to find food, he plunged into his rucksack and drew out most of the contents. He found a tin of sardines, but he could not open it as his fingers were stiff and clumsy. Finally he took a piton and smashed a hole in the lid with it. We were both salivating heavily, and as soon as the lid was curled back we scooped out oily handfuls of fish and crammed them into our mouths. We swallowed them without chewing them. When we were sure that the tin was empty we let it fall out into the night.

Afterwards we divided some chocolate which I swallowed at once. I could feel its corners score painfully down my gullet.

Hansi's voice shook like a diseased man's. 'We must have warmth,' he said, 'we're too cold and too wet.'

He went back out onto the crag to collect some snow. It took several attempts before the heater stayed alight, and at that altitude the water took an age to boil. Eventually, however, we had enough to make several cups of tea. So much sugar was poured into these that they tasted sweeter than any drink I had ever had. A slurry of undissolved grains was left at the bottom of each aluminium cup, and we used our fingers to push it into our mouths. Beneath the sweetness I could still taste fish oil.

Afterwards we began to repack our rucksacks, and were so confused that we merely crammed things into them. Only when I had closed the flap did I realise that I had taken the sample jar from Hansi's pile and put it into my own sack. I wondered about opening the flap again to throw out the jar, but somehow this seemed as if it would be an infinitely wearying action to take.

Hansi had been licking his fingers free of food. 'Ernest,' he said, quite calmly, 'you have the lantern, don't you?'

For a few panic-stricken seconds I thought that I had lost it, but then it was found and held so that the beam fell on Hansi's fingers.

They looked bigger than usual, and had a bruised sheen, as if they had been jammed in a door. The third finger of the left hand was encircled by a purplish, oily thickness, as if the flesh had swollen around the bone.

'Can you bend them?' I asked.

Hansi flexed his hands, but had great difficulty with the left. 'I knew I was taking a chance,' he said.

I stared at the finger as if I could see the rot spread as I watched.

'My weak spot,' he said, and suddenly a tear rolled down his face and splashed on his clothes. I leaned over and embraced him. Even through the thickness of his clothes I could sense his chest heave as he cried.

After a minute or so he pulled away, his streaked face glistening in the flickering light. 'I'm sorry,' he said, and breathed deeply. 'That was foolish.'

I found another pair of his gloves and placed them on his hands as gently as I could. 'Hansi,' I said, 'I owe my life to you.'

'Don't think of such things. You would have done the same.'

'I hope so,' I said.

And I knew that, like me, he suspected that this would be our last resting-place, and that we would die here, wretched and alone, with no one to know where we were, and no one ever to find us.

'I dislike your friends,' I told her. 'I dislike their narrow interests, because they think of them as wide. I dislike their provincialism, because they see themselves as cosmopolitan. I don't like the way they make their money, and I don't like the way they spend it.'

On many occasions she had told me that she was bored and annoyed by them. Now, possibly because my attack was so planned, she was quick to their defence.

'They're bank managers, merchants, farmers, mill owners,' she said. 'And some of us haven't had the advantages you grew up with. What right have you to say such things?'

'I have a right to say what I think.'

She looked at me scornfully. 'Ernest, you're worse than they are. At least we have the money to support our snobberies and our pettiness. What have you got? You're not wealthy any more – you don't even own your own home. Look at this room. It's so grubby and ill-kept that I feel like getting down on my knees and scrubbing it out myself. You tell me your job has no prospects – and what kind of job is it? Do you create wealth, do you employ people who are in real need of a living wage? Not you. You comment on dead writers, you teach a foreign language, and that's it. Even your pleasures are solitary ones; climbing must be a lonely activity. You may not like what my friends do, but at least they create money, security, maybe even prosperity. They make it possible for people like you to make comments that are thoughtless and unfair.'

I started to protest, but she interrupted me.

'I know what you're going to say; that you're a world-class climber. Fine. But does that *matter*? What good will you have done when you step on the top of a remote peak? How will you have increased the prosperity of the world? How will you have *affected* it?'

'Easy,' I said. 'I'm demonstrating skill, and trust, and re-liability. Hansi and I must depend totally on each other. Neither of us would ever let the other down. That's an achievement, and an understanding, that wouldn't be possible among *your* friends. They would betray each other without a second thought. How do you stand living among them?'

She almost spat at me. 'What alternative is there?' she asked, so ferociously that I fell silent.

I glanced across at the sideboard. That very afternoon, a letter had arrived from Hansi. If Jean had followed my eyes, she would have seen the Swiss stamp. But, as she quietened, she stared instead at the books on the shelves.

'I have no income,' she said after a while. 'I have to rely on what Harry gives me. I have no education, no profession. My parents raised me as the kind of girl that someone like Harry would want to settle down with. I have no independence at all. If I ever have children I shall have even less.'

'You mustn't underestimate yourself,' I said.

'I don't. But I don't misjudge my dependence, either. *I* can't

105

choose, Ernest. I have to take what seems like the best bargain, the most secure offer. If I didn't, I would starve. Or I'd finish up being a waitress or a chambermaid. You think that money protects me. It's like a rug that could be pulled out from under my feet.'

'But you must *like* these people.'

'Sometimes, yes. A lot of the time I don't think about it. I have to live among them, so I have to find ways of making the best of what I've got.'

'You mean you'd go along with things, perhaps things you didn't like, just for the sake of a roof over your head or three square meals a day?'

'So would you, if you were in my position.'

I drew in my breath, and felt it swell my chest before I exhaled. 'Jean,' I said.

She looked at me. I wished she had not.

'I'm leaving,' I said.

'Leaving?' Her voice had become small, and it trembled.

I spoke in rapid, short sentences, wishing to justify myself quickly. 'It's time I got away. I've talked about it often enough. I was thinking of going on holiday anyway. Now I think I should leave permanently. I could get a job teaching English. And climb at weekends.'

'You're going back to Switzerland?'

'I belong there. You saw that a long time ago.'

'Yes.'

I nodded at the letter. 'That came today. From Hansi. He's been involved in a rescue on the Eiger. He says that it has made him determined to climb a north face. Just like if you're involved in a driving accident you should always get back into the car.'

She shook her head.

'There's a mountain called the Versücherin – you know what that means?'

'No.'

106

'Temptress. Its north wall has never been climbed before. And time is running out.'

'Is that important?'

'More than you realise. The letter's there; read it if you wish. I must write an answer tonight.'

She shook her head again.

'You'll read about me in the papers,' I said.

She did not understand.

'When I get to the top,' I explained.

'Take me with you,' she said.

I had considered the possibility that she might ask, but rejected it as unlikely. Nevertheless I laughed uneasily. I had not expected her request to be made in such a forthright manner.

'I can't,' I said.

'Why not?'

'You're not serious. I know you're not.'

'I could be your helper,' she said with a sudden, fiery enthusiasm.

'What?'

'I could stay at the bottom and do whatever helpers do. Carry your things. Signal to you. Feed you when you came back, wash your hair, bathe your bruises.'

She had such an expression in her eyes that I could not really believe that she knew what she was saying.

'Jean, this isn't the same as a weekend away. I'm going for a long time. Years. Perhaps forever. You can't sacrifice your marriage for a casual affair. What have you just been talking about? Harry wouldn't stand for it, he'd cut you off without a penny.'

'Don't you think that's what I should do?'

'Jean –'

'I wasn't meant for Harry. Now that you've met him, you must realise that.'

I said nothing.

'Don't you agree that I should be irresponsible, kick over the

107

traces, be an enemy to my own interests? I could be different. I could be free. I could be *someone else*.'

I watched her, startled by her passion. Outside a cloud passed across the sun. In the dimmed light her eyes still shone.

'I would have very little money,' I said tentatively.

'When it runs out, I *could* be a waitress. Or perhaps, like you, I could teach English?'

'Perhaps.'

I sat pondering the future. Her energy and passion hung in the space between us, charging it.

A short while later I wrote my letter to Hansi. The Kurz affair must have been terrible, I said; was he sure that the frostbite would be healed within the next few weeks? The Versücherin north, if we were to do it, would need all our fitness, strength, confidence.

Then I told him I was thinking of returning to Switzerland to live. And I added:

I must tell you that I may not be alone when I join you at the Seematters'. I may have a companion. Her name is Jean. I'm not absolutely certain about this, but she wants to come with me, even if it means sacrificing all she now has. I'll tell you more when we meet. I hope you will understand the position I'm in, and not be offended. Of course, this won't affect our partnership in any way at all. And it won't affect our climb. My intentions haven't changed, and neither has my ability. After we've stood on the summit (I'll not consider a retreat!) I shall think about Jean, and what I should do about

I stopped. I was going to write *our affair*, but decided against it. Instead, I finished the paragraph with the words *my friendship with her*. Then I sealed the envelope and posted it as swiftly as I could, so that I would not have the opportunity to alter it.

*

The night was one of aching discomfort and repeated, frustrated attempts at sleep. I had no idea what the time was, and my misery was increased by a savage thirst which overtook me in the early hours and would not lessen its grip until we could make more tea on another cold, grey morning. My mouth tasted as if it had been smeared with salt, and my fingers were so numb that I had to rub them, again, with fresh snow before sensation crept back into them.

Once more we had to struggle to light the heater; once more it appeared that it would never give enough heat to boil the snow. Hansi was ashen, although beneath his eyes was a greenish tinge. I wondered if I, too, looked as bad as this, a creature of stubble, lined skin, sunken eyes.

Everything was sluggish – the flame, our movements, our speech. Even the clouds, trailing tendrils over the wall, did not move. I stared at the heater flame as it wavered; I listened to the sleety drip of water within the cave; I fell asleep.

A sudden agonising nervous spasm jerked me awake. Nothing had altered even though I felt I had lost consciousness for several minutes. A wispy trail of vapour hung around the heater, and Hansi still had not moved. He lay with his gloved hands tucked beneath his armpits, the altimeter hanging from his neck on a cord. For a moment I thought that he had died.

'Hansi?' I asked, in a brittle croak.

His eyes opened and he looked at me.

'Let me see your hands,' I demanded.

When we had removed the gloves it was obvious that the bad finger had worsened considerably through the night. It looked greasily black, unnatural, hardly like a human finger at all. Somewhere I could feel my mind trying to grasp this enormity.

'You need urgent treatment, my friend,' I said, as lightly as I could.

'I'll lose that one anyway,' he answered; 'it's the others I'm worried about.'

I nodded, but could think of nothing else to say. I did not even want to consider the problem. All I wanted was warmth, a freshly made bed to curl up in, and Jean. If I really put my mind to it, I could summon up a cosy scene of my recovery from the climb. Lavender would be placed on the balconies, white lace curtains would sway in a warm breeze, the Seematters would be as faithful and solicitous as servants, Jean would smooth my hair and feed me as if I were a sickly child. Perhaps, even, the world's press would be gathered at my door, eager for interviews and photographs.

'We have enough food for today,' Hansi continued, forcing his way through the consequences of our predicament like a man clearing a path through thorns, 'and we need energy before we can do much else.'

I stared at the cave mouth, and at the screen of icicles which had grown like a curtain across its upper edge.

Hansi took one hand in the other and pushed back the top of his balaclava, as men did with hat-brims when they wished to think. The fringe of matted hair that showed beneath it was like the fur of a drowned animal. 'We must eat what we can,' he went on doggedly, 'and not be wasteful or foolish. And then we must attempt to get out of here. You must lead, Ernst, because my fingers will be no good.' As he spoke he ran the back of his hand along his chin, so that the bristles rasped on his knuckles.

'All right,' I agreed, but my voice was thin and fragile.

We opened a tin of condensed milk and drank it without pouring it into the mugs. I scarcely noticed how sickly it tasted, or how jagged the metal was on my lips. After this we ate more chocolate, but by now cold had hardened the bars so much that they were difficult to snap and could not be bitten through. We sat and softened them in our mouths, the saliva running unchecked down our chins.

We drank tea until all the water had gone, then struggled to

110

urinate outside the cave. Our urine was thick, yellow, and smelled of ammonia.

Every so often, Hansi peered at the altimeter.

'How far?' I asked at last.

'It's difficult to tell. There may be a depression still above us. But it can't be far.'

'Perhaps we should stay here,' I suggested, my heartbeat increasing at the thought.

He shook his head. 'Even if there *is* a rescue team, the chances of them getting to us in time are too slim.'

Outside the cloud was still thick on the wall, but the wind had dropped and only a few squalls of snow scattered across the crag.

It took me a long time to rope up and by the time I had stepped out on to a pitch of black rock, the wind had almost ceased. I had no confidence; all that had gone. The Versücherin was a never-ending puzzle, a vertical maze thick with false trails and dead ends and fatal traps. Its complexity would always elude our understanding; we were doomed to live out the end of our short lives here.

I climbed in a silence that was so profound that I could hear the click of my boots, the rustle of my hardened clothes as I dragged myself up the fragile surface, the murmur of rock slivers as I pushed them away when I took hold.

Higher, and the rock became firmer. At the top of the pitch it levelled into a dome of frozen snow which led to a number of gullies packed with greyish ice. To either side the wall was precipitous, without holds. I peered at the upper reaches of the gullies but could not see beyond them. Gradually, however, I began to realise that these were part of a series that projected from the face like teeth from a saw. Hansi and Max had looked down on them from the summit.

Quite suddenly I began to hope again, but when I looked more closely at the gullies I saw that they were set within a rock overhang. The mountain was tormenting us once more.

111

I yanked at the rope and Hansi fed more slack up to me. The pitons clinked as I selected one, and I could hear a tiny grating whisper as I scored the ice with its tip. When I hammered it home the blows echoed round the crags like the striking of a smith's anvil. I fixed a snap-link, heard its satisfying click, and pushed the rope through.

When I took a few more steps onto the ice dome I could hear a ghostly creak as it took my weight. I raised my hands and pushed the balaclava back from my ears. From very far away, and with an oddly unreal quality, I could hear a rising, falling, interleaved sound, like voices raised in conversation.

I stepped further up the ice, but my crampons bit loudly enough to drown out any further noise. I had to stand as still as I could for several seconds before I could listen again. Even then my heart was beating with an unnatural loudness, and the breath was noisy in my throat.

Even fainter, the sound came again.

I opened my mouth and shouted as loudly as I could, but my voice was too weak to carry far, and its echoes quickly died. Above me the cloud, bruised and flowing thickly, spilled across the top of the gullies.

I slithered back to the piton and began smashing it with my hammer to produce an artificial, rhythmic signal. I could hear Hansi shouting up at me, but I did not have time to listen. The piton disappeared under the ice and the dome began to sink into a murky gloom as the cloud closed around it. I glanced round feverishly as it closed in, but I could see and hear nothing more.

I swung myself back onto the upper reach of the pitch. All around me the air was snapping and crackling as if huge sheets of cellophane were being crumpled, and my clothes lifted in an eerie levitation. My scalp felt as if hundreds of tiny insects were crawling round each hair, and my face was tensed. The muscles had contracted and drawn the lips back from my teeth.

The metal link began to crackle with spectral fire, and suddenly I was covered in a net of dancing light as the electricity flared on my clips, hammer, pegs. I slid down the rope, the net fading around me like a vanishing mirage. High on the gullies lightning and thunder burst out in a series of incandescent, deafening attacks.

Hansi touched my ankles as I neared the cave, although he could not hold me, merely steady me.

No sooner was I back inside than hailstones, bigger than I had ever seen, began to pound the face. Some bounced into our shelter, but none hit us directly. Unable to talk for the din, unable to see but for the chill luminescence of the hail, we huddled together like lovers while all around us was scoured and lashed.

It was a long time, perhaps an hour, before I could make myself heard. I had tried to tell Hansi several times, but he had not understood my gestures or my mime. His eyes gazed at me like a beaten dog's. At last, when the storm had lessened, I could talk, but I had spent the last hour thinking that even the best would have died in conditions like that.

'We're not far,' I said, 'and I don't think we're alone.'

'A rescue?'

'I don't know. Surely the Italians wouldn't have started under conditions like this.'

'I don't know. Maybe. They would be a stronger team than us. But conditions like this would have beaten anyone back.' He sat silent for a while. 'Ernst,' he said at last, 'did you imagine it?'

'I can't be sure,' I confessed.

'If it *is* a rescue party, they must have come up by the east ridge. They could be waiting for us with food, stretchers.'

'In a storm like this? They would have gone back to your hut, the one with all the mice.'

Hansi tugged off his glove and stared at his bad hand. The skin was deadening by the hour, and the third finger had begun to lose its outer skin, which slid away to show the shiny blackness beneath. 'I don't think Max Volkwein would find us photogenic now,' he said, attempting a joke.

'No.'

'This is going fast, Ernst. If we ever get off here, I could lose most of it. What would be my future then, do you think?'

'You would adapt.'

'If I lost most of my fingers, perhaps them all? It is poisoning me quickly. The other hand will start to rot soon. I have never fully recovered from the Eiger. That has been my failure. I bear the responsibility for this.' He gestured in the air to indicate our position on the mountain.

'You could still teach.'

'A teacher of sport, in a condition like mine?'

'They could be saved,' I said weakly.

Neither of us spoke for several minutes. Hailstones, a little smaller than before, bounced near to our feet, but their force was spent and they were not dangerous. The icicles at the cave mouth had lengthened. I wondered if we would die there and, like sleepers in a magic cave, be sealed forever within the mountain.

'Max is a committee member for one of the Leader Schools,' Hansi said after a while.

I looked at him. I did not know why he was telling me this.

'He is very famous; they are delighted to have him,' he went on. 'They value his opinion.'

'Yes?'

'And they need someone who is a good Alpine man.'

'As a teacher? Hansi, you couldn't go there.'

'Why not?' he asked, a touch of anger in his voice. 'My father was German, and Max says that would help. And he says, too, that *he* would do what he could for me. Apparently my chances are excellent, anyway. But if we conquered the north wall –' He stopped, then added, 'If I was a complete man, of course.'

'They need someone like you?'

'It's for the élite. I would live very near Munich.'

I was stunned. When we had talked a year or so ago, Hansi had been dismissive of the entire German system. Now he was daydreaming about working within its very core.

As if he anticipated my objection, he began to justify himself. 'It would allow me to do what I want to do, Ernst. They would give me the time, and the money, to develop my talents. I could even climb in other parts of the world. I could become *world class*. Agreeing with Max and his friends is a small price to be asked to pay.'

He stared at his hand and touched it, gingerly, with the other. Part of the skin slipped down the third finger, like the sloughed skin of a reptile.

'Besides,' he continued, 'there comes a time when a man must change his views. The tide has turned in favour of Max. Everyone saw that at the Olympics. Why should I remain outside? I love my country, Ernst, but whatever happens it will always remain neutral, always be on the edge of things.' He was quiet for a while, then spoke again. 'It will always be *safe*,' he said.

'You couldn't remain detached in a Leader School, Hansi. You wouldn't be allowed just to say you agree with them; you'd have to prove it.'

'All right, I would prove it. If they wanted me to.'

'You'd do what? Swear allegiance? Toe the party line? Talk about blood and soil and destiny and will? Preach that each climb you made was a proof of the aristocracy of the spirit?'

'Isn't it?' he asked sharply.

'No,' I said.

He shook his head as if I were a recalcitrant child. His mouth cracked in a smile that would have been tolerant had it had not been constricted by his discomfort and fatigue. 'We are different from ordinary men. We strive for things that are far above the ordinary and the limited. When we get out of this, you should talk with Max a lot more than you have done. You would see things much more clearly.'

'Hansi, you always were something of a chameleon.'

Beneath his coat he tried to shrug. Then he extended the frostbitten hand towards me. 'Perhaps. But I have always had a better grasp of realities than you. It is obvious to me that we dare not spend another night here. We must leave now, and brave the worst.'

'And die on the next section?'

'Better to die struggling than to await death like the defeated.' He looked straight at me, studied me, and unexpectedly said, 'Your eyebrows have been singed. Did you know?'

'No.' The electrical storm, I supposed. 'You don't look too good yourself,' I added, as wryly as I could.

He tried to laugh, but it came out as a croak. 'Ernst, you and I have always been the best of friends. We must find a way out of this together, yes?'

'We can't do anything. Not just yet.'

'But we *must* do. We must move out onto the face. Look, the snow is easing.'

'I don't see it.'

'And before we go, you must amputate this finger.'

I looked hard at him. 'You don't mean it.'

'I do. I would do it myself, but the other hand is too clumsy.'

'I won't do it, Hansi. It's insane.'

'On the contrary, it is necessary. I can watch the rot spread. Before it goes any further, it must be removed. Otherwise I will lose the others, too; without this one, I still have a chance.'

I was cold at the very thought of it, and involuntarily drew away from him.

'With just one finger gone I can still hang onto the rope. But if we survive, if we succeed, what use is a climber with a finger-less hand? Where are my chances at the Leader School then?'

'We may be back in the valley in a couple of days. They –'

'It won't wait.'

116

'I'm still not going to mutilate you.'

He reached out with his good hand and touched me lightly on the cheek. 'For the sake of our friendship, Ernst.'

I could hear the wind sigh, then drop, outside.

'It's my fault that you're like this,' I said angrily. I was furious at the workings of chance, at our bad luck, our wrong decisions. I was furious that Hansi had been able to save me only by using his bare hands. 'All right,' I said, and searched for my knife.

Hansi did not thank me, but merely placed his hand flat on the cave floor. Where the skin had peeled away, the third finger of his left hand glistened with a dark liquid.

I tested the blade for sharpness.

'It will do,' he said reassuringly, 'I'll not feel a thing.'

I spread the fingers with the point of the blade. If I could have operated with my eyes closed, I would have done.

'Are you ready?' I asked, and he nodded. Where I had touched the finger with the knife point, there was still an impression. It carried an indentation as rotten wood can carry the print of a thumb.

I severed the finger rapidly, cutting it at the lower knuckle. The knife passed easily through the flesh, and separated the bones with a tiny click. I pulled away the blade and could see only a smear of blood.

Hansi sat back, breathed out, and seemed to relax. 'You would have made a good surgeon, Ernst,' he said. But I knew he would have said that even if I had botched the amputation.

I pointed at the severed finger with my knife, not daring to touch it. Now that it was no longer part of a body, I was repelled by it. 'What about this?' I asked.

Hansi looked at it for a few seconds and then, with a rapid movement, tried to sweep it from the cave with his arm. The finger rolled a few inches, and he had to make several sweeps with his arm before it finally disappeared over the rim.

As soon as it had vanished he leaned over and tried to vomit, but could not. I closed my eyes and sat with the knife still gripped in my fist.

Two days before we left, Jean opened a notebook, unscrewed a pen, and looked at me like an efficient secretary waiting to take dictation. 'What should I say to Harry?' she asked.

I was amazed. 'I don't know what you should say. That's your responsibility.'

'Yes, but I need your help.'

'This is absurd,' I protested. 'How can I tell you what you should write?'

She looked hurt and disappointed.

'Just say goodbye,' I suggested.

'He deserves more than that.'

I shrugged. 'I'm sorry, but I don't really think it's up to me to advise you.'

'You're the one who knows about literature. You can quote all kinds of fine phrases. I need professional advice.'

I came to a decision. 'All right. What do you want to say? That you're leaving him for me? That we're going to start a new life together in a place he'll never find? If so, then put it down simply, directly, so there can be no doubt in his mind. I'll correct the grammar.'

'Ernest, I want to say much more than that.'

'You'd only be making things more difficult for yourself.'

'It's essential,' she replied sharply.

Neither of us spoke for a few seconds.

'I must tell him that I love him,' she said.

I could scarcely believe what I had just heard. 'Love?' I repeated, foolishly.

'Oh, I know that you would prefer to think that I don't. But I do. Of course our life is unsatisfactory, of course I'm leaving him. But he'll be injured by my escape. It'll hurt his pride and his dignity. I owe him a decent farewell.' She was silent for a while, then she went on. 'I should have the courage to tell him to his face, but I can't do that.'

'And me?' I asked, unable to disguise my resentment. 'What about me?'

She kissed me even though I tried to pull away. 'Don't be foolish, Ernest. You've never been in Harry's shoes, and perhaps you never will be. I get things from you that I've never had from him.'

I was determined to hear more of this. 'Such as?' I asked.

'Oh, lots of things.'

'Yes?'

'Excitement. Knowledge. A sense of wider horizons, frontiers. Europe. I don't really feel English, Ernest. I was born here, I live here and was married here, but I don't feel as if I belong. It's as if I was a changeling.'

'Until you met me you'd never heard of such a thing.'

'Exactly. I learned about investment and return, the hierarchy of local class and family, all the paraphernalia of county matters and manners. For years I was supported by that, and I even pretended that it nourished me. But we both know that I needed something else, something which you have given me. Now, please, let us decide what I should say to Harry.'

We began to consider alternatives.

After much discussion, and several drafts, Jean was able to copy out a letter in a steady, calm script.

My dearest Harry,

By the time you have opened this letter you must have guessed the truth – that I have left you forever. I have spent a long time coming to this decision, and I have only reached it after much heart-searching and some pain. Now that the future has been decided I have acted in the swiftest way possible to make a clean break. Do not try to find me, for I shall not even be in this country.

I am going with Ernest Tinnion. I recognise that you will be distressed by this, but please try not to feel humiliated. You have nothing to reproach yourself for – you have been a good husband, considerate and kind, and have given me every comfort. It should not surprise you that I have chosen to turn my back on such fine qualities. You have known about my dissatisfaction for some time. That I now choose uncertainty, and run the risk of public shame, you can ascribe to my ambitious and unsettled heart.

I want to tell you that I love you. If you know me deeply, you will not find that a paradox. I shall always be grateful to you, and when I think of you my memories will be fond ones. But love is not enough – or, at least, our kind of love is not.

Do not reproach yourself. Blame me for everything. Please take care of yourself and, if you must, forget me.

Jean signed the letter carefully, still giving a flourish to her signature.

I was both discomfited and pleased. I did not wish her to praise me in the letter, but nevertheless I felt slighted that she had not. I did not think that our affair would last the rest of our lives. She had not said it would, and I expected her to. I thought the letter would be one of justification and expediency, but Jean had been concerned with the truth.

Afterwards she would not make love, as I wanted to. Instead she insisted that I remove the wedding-ring from her finger.

'You'll be better off wearing it,' I said, 'it will cause less suspicion on our travels.'

'It goes in the letter to Harry,' she insisted. 'I'll buy the cheapest one I can find as a replacement. That will be enough. I must learn to be poor now.'

She extended her hand.

'Are you sure?' I asked, and she nodded.

I was not used to dealing with rings, so my movements were clumsy. I could not get the ring past the larger knuckle. For a moment I thought it was fastened so tightly to her finger that only a hacksaw or amputation would free it.

'Push the finger upwards,' she said; 'there, like that.'

The ring slid off easily. I held it in my hand.

'Give it to me,' she said. I passed it over and she clenched it within her fist.

I was dazed by the speed and drama of events, and tried to force myself into believing that she would really come with me. Doubts continued to nag at me, however, and I conjured up all kinds of reasons why she would not take that last irrevocable step. And, because I had never been able to make a clean break myself, I had neither the heart nor the courage to dispose of my own few possessions. They had been boxed and put into store. Only when I saw Jean walking down the platform towards me did I know that my life had changed in ways that were still mysterious.

We sat beside each other in the train, our hands clasped together. As the engine gathered speed I felt its heavy velocity, as balanced as a dancer, carrying us into a new world. I was happy and slightly stunned, and congratulated myself on my attractiveness and worldliness.

Jean was unable to speak, and looked out of the window as white clouds of racing smoke lifted from a view of ripening fields and, miles away, a faint line of hills. After a while she took a tiny handkerchief from her handbag and dabbed her eyes with its corners.

The cloud had thinned, and in places it had parted to reveal a late afternoon sky that was tranquil and clear. We were sprawled across the entrance to our shelter. I looked up with aching, weary eyes, feeling that I was a dreamer under opium seeing an impossible mirage. My mind became absurdly energetic but without direction, so that my thoughts spun like a wheel sprung free of its drive. The cloud gaps closed again, and the sky became a thin translucent sheet, as if it was a delicately woven material which disintegrated as we watched. Soon all the cloud was dispersing, and above it, astonishing, brilliant, was a heaven of pure, endless blue.

Gradually, like men being granted a vision, we moved out on to the rock, our faces turned upwards. There was even, we believed, a slightly warmth to the moist, rich, giddying air. We could feel it on our cracked lips and crusted skin.

Everything was still.

I do not know how long we hung there on the side of the crag. Eventually Hansi spoke. 'We have to go now,' he said.

I looked at him. There was a surface shine to his eyes, as if a film had grown across them. 'We'll never make it in daylight,' I said. I looked at my watch and found that I could not read it. I knew that it was working, for when I held it next to my ear I could hear the tick, but no matter how hard I struggled I could not understand the position of the hands.

'How many hours have we got?'

'Three,' I decided at last, 'perhaps four.'

'If we could reach the summit cairn, there are our stores.'

'We would die well-fed, then.'

For some reason we found this to be hysterically funny, and we both began to laugh, although the noises resembled breathless yelps and ended as suddenly as they had begun. When Hansi had stopped laughing the grin remained on his face. His skin had the look of putty with a greenish tinge, and his teeth resembled pieces of yellow ivory. I thought of the altar Max had taken us to see.

'Check the knots, will you, Ernst? I can no longer do it.'

I told him they were all right. 'You'll have no difficulty with a fixed rope,' I said, 'but we should try to recover it.'

'Forget it, Ernst. We'll leave it where it is.' The smile gave a twitch. 'We must forget technique. We have little left to lose. Let's begin.'

We moved up the black rock, our lungs rasping like files across metal, whilst all the time the sky remained open and blue.

Hansi came up the rope quite easily, but I had to grasp the cloth of his jacket and tug him on to the ice dome. When his footing was safe he looked at me, confused, then peered down the crag.

'Hansi?' I asked.

He glanced at me, then looked back down. 'I thought there was someone else,' he said.

I could not understand what he meant.

'I thought there was a third man on the rope,' he said. Before I could respond, he spoke again. 'You needn't tell me, Ernst, I know now that there is not.'

Our eyes met, and then he looked away. We both understood that he was failing.

I walked across the dome with slow and glutinous movements. When I looked at the gulley straight ahead of me I could see that the ice within it was bulbous and erratic. I had never seen ice like that. Hansi came shambling after me.

We reached the base of the gulley. I touched its rock, which was layered like a huge column of black tiles. Ice filled all the crevices and coated all the ledges. Within the gulley walls the ice was packed, hollowed, puzzling. Here was no simple flume, but a jungle of cornices, plateaus, grottoes, each with surfaces of oily whiteness or crystalline glitter.

'The storm,' Hansi said.

At last I understood that it had been a bolt of lightning which had transformed our escape route into a series of baroque ice sculptures crammed one on top of the other. It was a climb impossible to judge.

'This is madness,' I said.

'You must break through,' Hansi insisted wearily.

I turned to him. 'I can't. The mountain is against us. Look – it is as if this had been designed to trap us.'

'Design? No, heat and rapid cooling, that's all. The lightning must have gone down it, like it goes down the trunk of a tree.'

I felt my knees buckle, and I leaned against the rock to stop myself from falling. 'We can climb this in the morning, Hansi. It would be safer.'

If he had agreed, I would have sunk down onto the ice and curled up in sleep. I knew that I would never wake up, and I did not care.

'We must do this now, Ernst. And you must lead.'

'We can't,' I said.

He took a step nearer to me and brandished his axe. It was a motion so clumsy that it lacked all menace. He held the axe in the air for a moment then let it fall.

I felt the shock elsewhere in my mind, like a distant tremor. 'All right,' I said, and turned to the gulley. All around us the mountain grew colder and darker.

It was an endless, stupefying struggle. I had to use pitons, and I kept dropping them so that they shot away and disappeared forever. Hansi's dexterity had grown more cramped and, although he could brace himself, I had to haul him upwards inch by inch. With one piton I grew so confused that I did not know how to fix it. I put the metal to my lips and yanked it away just in time, before it froze to the scab that had formed.

Once among the formations I became more and more convinced that they were the work of some directed force. Here was a designed assembly of problems, a torture garden of ice. There were chimneys with transparent, water-white walls so cellular that they could be punched through; turrets with melted castellations, like confections of sugar; tiny, geometric apertures like the blowholes of submarine mammals; grottoes with recesses as green as the bottoms of wine bottles. I wormed, scrambled, smashed through them, the lobsterclaws screeching on their delicate surfaces.

Towards the end I came to an elaboration of wafer-thin ice spun across my path. It resembled an insects' nest of glass, or an intricate chandelier, and within it rainbows faded and died. I broke into it at its lowest point. All its filaments came apart, and tumbled past me in a rattling cascade.

The gulley opened onto an angled icefield that had been polished by wind. I rested on one of the rock spurs at its base, then dragged Hansi after me. He came to the surface like a blind and wounded animal. I thought of letting go of the rope, and simply forgetting him.

We lay together at the foot of the icefield, our feet projecting over the gulley, and a jumble of stiffened rope curled round us like a trap. I ran my finger across the surface and could find no flaw; the ice was as smooth as a lens. Above us the last moments of sunlight caught the field, making it flare with a cold brilliance. The glare was reflected on Hansi's face.

'Check the angle,' he said.

Half-heartedly, I struck the rock with my hammer. Nothing came away, and I had to strike again before we got a large enough piece. When I tossed it onto the icefield it slithered back more slowly than I would have thought possible.

'We're there,' he said.

I looked dumbly at the icefield.

'There is no gradient like this until the last few metres. We're there.'

'Could you be wrong?'

'I've studied this from the summit. I'm right – we have this, and that's all. Once we have climbed it, we are there.'

I felt neither elation nor pride, merely a kind of stunned acceptance. The north wall no longer seemed important.

'You must still lead, Ernst. I'm no good at all now.'

125

But I would not move.

'Bear to the left; that is the best route.'

I tried to speak, but could not.

'Ernst,' he urged me, 'you *must* do this.'

And now it did indeed seem to me that we were doomed men, condemned to labour forever on the slopes and precipices of the Temptress. We were no longer ourselves, but figures in a ritual, marionettes on a heartless, bleak, vertical stage. All the things that had given us identity had been stripped away. I had become a mere assemblage of muscle, sinew, bone. I was a pattern of reactions to stimuli, an animal in a maze without a solution. I cut the steps because I knew I had to do them. I pushed myself inch by inch up the slippery grey surface because I had trained myself to do that, and nothing more. I dragged the rope behind me because that was part of the scheme, but I did not know why. I forced myself to remember that there was someone else at the end of the rope, but often I did not know who. The summit was nowhere in sight. I was not surprised. I merely expected this to go on, with neither victory nor resolution, until time itself dragged to a stop.

Quite suddenly everything changed.

The surface, which I had been staring at from close range, jolted, blurred, and began to move rapidly past me. I was dimly aware of a noise like small grains being poured from a bowl. I realised that I must be falling, but immediately I remembered the peg I had just fixed. That would hold me.

The ice careered out of my vision and I was looking at a darkening sky. There was still a sense of juddering motion.

I knew that the peg must have come away.

The ice yawed back into view, and chips of it showered against my face. I flailed at its surface with my axe, but the blade rebounded. Only at the fourth attempt did it cut into the ice, and by then I was accelerating rapidly. The point raised a gritty scream from the ice, and I tried to force myself onto the body of the axe so that it would bite more deeply. Quite suddenly, we braked to a stop. There was a pain in my chest as if a huge weight had been attached to the lower end of the rope.

When I was motionless I searched frantically for another peg. The tension in the ropes began to pivot me around the axehead, and soon I was horizontal on the ice. My purchase on the axe, and the pressure I could apply to it, lessened all the time. I dared not look to see what had happened to Hansi.

Half an hour ago I would have fallen asleep in comfort; now the shock of the fall made me more alert than I had been for a long time. I was determined not to die like this.

Eventually, in a panic that saw no further than the next second, I hammered a peg into the ice just beside the rope, and managed to secure it with a snap-link. Just ahead of me, at the edge of my vision, was a rocky outcrop. The rope passed straight across it.

The silence was astonishing. I had expected that there would be shouts, although I had no idea who from. Perhaps I expected someone to call me and tell me not to worry, that I would soon be out of this. But all around me there was silence and the darkening mountain.

'Hansi?' I asked.

There was no reply.

'Hansi?'

I lifted my head as far as I could, then tried to ease my position on the ice. The rope was taut across the rock, and from its tension I guessed that Hansi must be suspended on the end of it. Only after repeated attempts did I succeed in moving my body so that I could see him.

The rope was lashed tightly around me, and the weight on it was such that I was allowed hardly any movement. As taut as a bowstring, it passed across the outcrop, and Hansi hung on its lower part so that it was as vertical as a plumb-line. He was a few feet away from the rock; close enough to touch it, if he had the strength.

I was splayed on the lip of the overhang like an abandoned sacrifice. 'Hansi, can you hear me?' I called.

'Yes.' His reply was surprisingly clear, yet distant.

'Have you broken anything?'

It took him a long time to answer. 'No,' he said.

'Can you get to the rock?'

He stretched out his hand, then let it fall.

'Hansi?'

Half-heartedly, he tried again.

'Hansi, you must get onto the rock and support your own weight. You must do it now.'

His arm flopped in a weary movement.

I scrambled as much as I could around my fixed point, trying to find a position where I could obtain enough leverage to haul Hansi upwards. Even as I did I wondered if a small increase in pressure, perhaps no more than an ounce, would spring the peg loose. The ice made strange noises as I turned upon it.

I had begun, now, to reason that if Hansi were a dead weight I would never be able to lift him. The pain in my chest became harsher, then tightened, making me breathe more quickly and with less depth. Below me Hansi was hanging, apparently relaxed, his arms and legs apart like a man floating in a buoyant sea.

I pushed myself along the icefield, wedging my body with the axe and kicking holds with the lobsterclaws, trying to use the link as a crude pulley. It was a hopeless task. I dared not stand, even if I had been able to, because then the outward force would have ripped the peg out of the ice. But tugging like that, half-recumbent, half-crouched, was the most difficult way to raise any weight.

Despite this I managed to pull, crawl, roll a few feet away from the ridge. I must have borne Hansi upwards in an uneven series of tiny, swaying lifts. At each moment I expected the line to slacken as, at last, he reached for the overhang and grasped it. But it never did.

I came to a halt. The rope was cutting into me and my breathing was hopelessly broken. I gazed up the gloomy icefield and at the stars which were appearing above it. It made me bitter and furious that everything was ending so absurdly, so helplessly.

Then I slid towards the peg – not much; a fraction, no more. I tried to find purchase with the axe, but could not. Like a sack of grain I was dragged back down the slope, rotating in an arc until I was brought up short against the peg.

I was in exactly the same position as I had been in before.

I lay face down, my legs splayed behind me. The peg and snap-link were right in front of my eyes. I could see the scratches on the metal, and watch a collar of ice form around it. And, if I lifted my head, I could see Hansi hanging, apparently unconcerned, at his end of the rope. Beneath him the valley floor was a thick grey colour, and it grew darker by the minute.

I hated him. I hated his optimism, his foolhardiness, his weakness, his naïvety. The pain in my chest had become so excruciating that I did not think I could stand it for more than a few minutes, and yet minutes passed, and I told myself I would endure it for just a little while longer. The pain and despair were so intense that I became racked with sobs, and teardrops froze in irregular spots in front of my face.

'Ernst?' Hansi called.

I could not answer.

But again, after a minute or so – 'Ernst?'

'What?' I asked in a drowning snarl.

His voice had an odd, contented tone, as if he was drifting off to sleep. 'When will you get me up? Soon?'

'Yes, soon.'

Nothing happened for a while, then he called again. 'You should find it easy. There are two of you, aren't there?'

'Yes, Hansi,' I said.

I took the ends of my gloves between my teeth and pulled them off. This took quite a long time. When my hands were bare I searched in my coat pocket for my knife. All sense had been lost in my fingertips, and it took me an age to find it.

When, at last, I had grasped it, I brought it carefully up the side of my body to just in front of my face. The blade had not been fully closed and the point protruded slightly from its recess in the handle. I could not lever it further, however, unless I lodged it against a thin layer of rock. Even then I took several attempts, each moving the blade marginally further, before I could snap it open fully.

Once open, the knife was difficult to hold. I fed it into my right hand by holding the blade with my left. As I did, I almost dropped it. Then I used my left hand to fold and tighten the grip of my right hand.

Swallowing nervously, I began to saw at the rope. I concentrated on the section just in front of my eyes. For a while I could not bear to look at Hansi, but when I did I saw that he was gazing straight upwards, as if he was unaware of what was happening.

The first few motions of the blade were misjudged, and passed harmlessly over the surface of the rope. But then I sliced a few strands, and they sprang out from the rope like growths reaching for light. I began to wonder if I could sever the rope cleanly and quickly; my hands were so numb that it seemed a difficult thing to do. I adjusted my grip to seek an angle which would be decisive. Hansi stared upwards with an expression of lazy pleasure on his face.

'Hansi?' I asked.

'Is that you, Ernst?'

I wanted to say something, but could not. I had loved him, but now I wanted to be rid of him. I could offer neither a justification nor a goodbye.

I closed my eyes and pressed as hard as I could with the blade, rocking it to and fro so that the cut would deepen quickly. But the knife, although it sliced into the hemp and lodged there, did not go deep enough. Not knowing how much pressure I was exerting, I forced it as hard as I could.

The handle slipped from my grasp.

I opened my eyes and saw the blade wedged within its incision, only a few inches away from my hand. Before I could reach it, the knife slipped from its hold and fell away with a silent, heart-stopping grace.

Hansi's head did not even turn as it sailed past him. I put my forehead on the ice and closed my eyes.

A long time passed. The pain in my chest eased, but most of my body seemed to have lost its sensitivity to feelings. As the night wore on my thoughts loosened and lost focus. Even though I fought against sleep, oblivion curled around me and warmed me, as stealthily as a cat. I no longer thought of the immediate, but cushioned myself in vague, hypnotically cosy thoughts that had no centre. A curious lightness filled my chest, as if it were as hollow as a ball and could float idly upwards had I not been harnessed to the ridge.

I could no longer make out the expression on Hansi's face, and for hours he was silent but for one cry.

'Rudi,' he shouted, 'come here and help me. Rudi.'

After that he said nothing else.

I twisted around and looked up at the sky. The night was full of stars. I was filled with wonder at their number and age, and I felt part of a huge, endless cycle, with all the evidence all around me, countless, untouchable, infinite.

In the early hours a shower of meteors passed across the stars, marking their path with thin scorings of light. Several crossed the entire sky before they vanished. I watched them, captivated and amazed. A delicious warmth began to inhabit me, and I dreamed that I was lying in a feather bed, so huge that its sides could not be found, so deep and soft that I had become lost within its welcome.

To keep myself awake I butted the end of the peg. I cracked one

tooth, filled my mouth with blood, and generated a fresh, jang-
ling pain that jerked me back from sleep. Now that I was on my
own I had no intention of giving in to the mountain.

Crab-like, I tilted myself so that I could gradually work the
rucksack from my back. I persevered for a long time, even though
it did not appear to be moving at first. When I finally had it by my
side I was bitterly regretting that I had not severed its straps with
my knife before I had attempted to cut the rope.

I hoped to be able to open the top flap easily, but I could not.
Instead I had to drag the rucksack in front of me and perch it on
the very edge of the drop. Then I tugged and pushed at the
straps until they were freed from their buckles. When it
was pushed back, the flap cracked with a noise like breaking
cardboard.

I searched inside. By now I had lost all sensation in my hands,
and I hardly knew what I was touching, so I pulled out all the
contents one by one. Some rolled or slid over the side of the crag.

Then, at last, I found the jar.

I withdrew it as delicately as I could, wedged it so it would not
move, and then I let go of the rucksack. I did not watch it fall, for
already I was twisting the neck of the jar.

My hand skidded uselessly over its curves; I would never be
able to open it like that.

I was tempted to let it fall, but I looked down at Hansi. His
figure floated motionless and ghostly against a velveteen blackness that had no depth at all. He was my anchorage and my
destroyer, and his very stillness mocked me.

'Hansi,' I said, but he did not reply.

I reached for the pitons that hung from my belt. They had
splayed into a fan and should have been easily detached, but I
had to rattle and tug at them until one slipped free.

I cupped the jar in my left hand, held the piton like a dagger in
my right, and jabbed at the lid. At first the point was deflected
and merely dented the metal, but after three or four attempts I

had punctured it. As if guiding a coupling, I slid the point back into the hole. Then by wrenching the piton back and forth, I widened the hole into a ragged gash.

Now I could wedge the peg within the lid and use it as a simple lever. Once or twice I lost my grip but gradually I rotated the jar's top until it unscrewed. The preservative fumes were so pungent that they made me blink.

Now I lifted the lid, and let it drop. The piton was placed beside the link that held us. Then, holding the jar as level as I could, I began to turn again on the ice. My clothes had frozen to it, and came away with a noise like glued plywood being torn apart. When I was in the best position, I raised the jar and poured the fluid into my mouth.

It was raw and sickening. It tasted of workbenches, paint-brushes, surgery. It burned down my throat, its trail searingly viscous, and some I had to cough out. But I forced myself to drink it all. The beetle legs caught in my throat and I could feel the wing cases as they slid down my gullet. Almost immediately I felt my heart begin to race, and the centre of my body warmed with a feverish, sickly heat.

Still holding the jar, I wriggled so that I was face down again. Then I smashed the glass by hammering it with the piton. A flying shard cut my cheek but I did not even blink. Finally, after further blows, I had my pick of several knife-sized slivers.

I picked the best, and extended my arms with the glass frag-ment held between my hands. I began to saw, right to left, left to right, across the cut I had begun with the knife. I did not look at Hansi, for I knew that this was my last chance and I needed to focus all my senses on the rope. But I knew he was there at the edge of my vision, hanging motionless.

The preservative made my heart thump loudly, terrifyingly. Although I worked as methodically as I could, there were mo-ments when I thought I would pass out. I had made a devil's pact; in return for a short period of warmth and energy, I had traded my health. Already the frozen capillaries would be rupturing.

As I worked, the sun came up. The sky was lighter, then it glowed and the far side of the valley became edged with streaks of brilliance. There was no wind, and all was silent but for my breath and the rasp of glass through hemp. Below me Hansi began to emerge from the gloom, and the clouds beneath him took on a rosy hue. His clothing was dappled by frost and his eyes were as bright as jewels.

The strands parted one by one. I watched the rest of the rope take up the tension. Around the cut the severed threads sprouted like the tendrils of an underwater plant.

Suddenly, as if it had come alive, the near section of the rope wriggled up towards me. Quietly, and without drama, Hansi's section vanished. One moment we were bound together by the rope, the next moment we were not. It was as simple as that. In a second, or less, he had disappeared as if he had vanished from the surface of the planet.

'Hansi,' I said.

All around was an endless icy silence.

I dropped the fragment of jar. Then I got up on all fours. It took me a long time to do it, for I was in an agony of cramp. When I had done this I forced my body into an ungainly crouch, then into a stoop. I tugged the rope out of the link and it hung from me like a severed halter.

The sun made the icefield glow. I started to climb it, trying to place the toes of my boots in the steps I had kicked the day before. Each step was painful, and I was unable to raise my head. After a few steps I had to vomit, and threw up alcohol and the remains of beetles onto the ice. My throat and tongue burned, and I could taste blood, too.

As the sun rose the plane of the icefield began to reflect it like a mirror. With neither goggles nor any form of shielding I became lost in an incandescence which blotted out all sense of direction.

All around me the light was furious and icy. My eyelids began to feel as if they had been gummed together, and at the same time it seemed that hot grit, like the ashes from a fire, had blown beneath them.

I could not tell if I was moving gradually upwards, staying where I was, or slipping back towards the cliffs. All I could smell was alcohol and, beyond that, the clear, clean tang of frozen snow; all I could hear were the sounds I made as I lashed at the ice with my crampons.

Even the last icefield was betraying me. No longer sure of its angle, unable to find reason within the crippled jumble of my senses, I stood motionless on its slope.

A hand reached out of the glare and caught me.

At first I would not believe it. But then, in a swirl of shadow and noise, other people moved around me, and oddly-pitched, urgent voices closed around me in a ring.

I squinted into a murky brightness, seeing shapeless masses form and part against the ice. I began to totter, and wanted to faint, but I knew that I was clasped steady. I was held straight even though my boots slid from beneath me.

My own name was being mentioned over and over again; I heard it, and felt it brush against me like a cushioned blow. I began to float upwards.

'Steady,' a voice said.

'Herr Tinnion,' a familiar voice said, 'you are almost at the top.'

'Otto?'

His voice was filled with pride and sorrow. 'We have waited for both of you,' he said.

'Let me stand,' I asked, and I was placed back in an upright position, although I sensed that hands were still outstretched if I should fall.

'Is there only you?' Otto asked.

'I can't see,' I said; 'what time is it?'

'Almost noon. We could not get here until now. Twice we were beaten back by the storm. We had to rest in the hut.'

Almost noon. I had spent several hours on the last icefield, unprotected from its glare.

'Ernst,' a voice asked. It was Max Volkwein's. 'What has happened to Hansi Kirchner? Is he still on the mountain?'

'Somewhere. I don't know where. Who else is here?'

The next time Max spoke, it was just in front of my face, as if he was staring at me from only a few inches away. 'Your eyes have been affected quite badly, I'm afraid. There is a small team of us. You have friends here.'

Someone spoke in rapid Italian. 'Bissolati?' I asked.

'I congratulate you,' Bissolati said in his heavy accent; 'all my men do. This is real –' He stopped, searching for the word.

'Courage,' Otto said.

There were several murmurings of agreement.

'And Herr Kirchner?' Otto asked. 'Is he still alive?'

'He can't be,' I said. I heard them all shuffle so that the crampons all made a sound like cogs biting. Somewhere within it there were several metallic clicks.

'The summit,' Max said, 'he must reach the summit. On his own.'

'He can hardly stand,' Otto protested.

'He can make it for the last few metres – can't you, Ernst?' Max spoke to me with a cold familiarity. 'We must be able to tell everyone that Ernst Tinnion got there on his own, unaided, by himself,' he went on.

There was a moment's silence. 'That is true already,' Bissolati said.

'Then we must be satisfied that it remains true to the last letter. There must be no doubt whatsoever. And we must be ready to swear it. Agreed?'

There were more murmurs of assent.

'Come then, Ernst,' Max said, like a ringmaster coaxing a

reluctant performer, 'there is really very little more space to cross.'

'I can't see. Am I facing in the right direction?'

'Yes,' Otto said, 'Follow me, I'll take you there.'

Again I began to walk uphill, but this time I was accompanied by a steady, reassuring crunch of boots, the occasional comment, and a sense of guidance. The light flickered and dimmed all around me. Bissolati asked if I wanted a pair of goggles, but I replied that it was already too late. Two or three times I was told to bear right because I was drifting from true. After a while I realised that the trailing rope was no longer being dragged behind me, but that it floated in the air in front of me, as if it had been charmed.

'Not much further,' Otto said, leading me by the severed rope. Then, a few feet later, he said proudly, 'This is *history*.'

The climb had ended.

At first I did not understand, for I found my way blocked by an irregular pyramidal shape that shielded part of the glare. I thought I would have to go round it, but Bissolati said, 'You're here,' and I reached out to touch the cairn. I could feel little but an indirect resistance along my upper arm. All the time I could hear, every few seconds, the same clicking as I had heard before.

I had done it. I was the first man up the Versücherin wall.

I had expected to be transformed by pride and achievement, but there was only a profound relief that my troubles were almost at an end. From round about came muffled clapping as glove struck glove, and a series of strange, spasmodic noises as my rescuers struck metal on metal, wood on leather.

'The book,' someone said.

I tried to nod. Someone began to chop ice mortar from the cairn.

'You will have to help me sign,' I said.

'I'll do that for you,' Otto said; 'it will be a privilege.'

'Wait,' I asked.

There was a pause. I attempted to imagine the men's expressions, for my snowblindness was such that I could not read them.

'I want to tell you what happened,' I said.

They waited.

'We fell. It was my fault.'

'Please,' Bissolati said, 'this is not a time for blame.'

'It's not a time for lies,' I said; 'it was *my fault*.'

They said nothing.

'Hansi was left hanging from the end of the rope. He was exhausted and didn't try to haul himself up. The only way I could get out of that was to cut the rope.'

'Herr Tinnion,' Otto began, but I held up my hand to silence him.

'He died at the end of the rope sometime during the night. By the time morning came he looked as if he had been dead for a long time. That was when I cut myself free. I wanted to do it when he was still alive, but I couldn't.'

The silence continued for a few seconds, then the noise of chopping came again from the cairn. It was followed by the sound of scrapes and thumps as the rocks were lifted.

Someone spoke in a cheerful Italian voice.

'He says your stores are still here,' Bissolati said lightly. 'At one time, the storm was so severe that we thought we might have to use them ourselves.'

'Didn't you hear what I said?' I asked.

He whispered confidentially in my ear. 'Say nothing more, Mr Tinnion. We all understand that you did what was necessary. Each of us would have done the same. Sometimes we must make sacrifices in order to survive.'

I reached out for Bissolati. I wanted to grab him so that I could repeat what I had said, but he embraced me like a favourite son.

'He was the only friend I've ever had,' I said fiercely.

'There,' he said, patting my back. His mouth was so close to my ear that only I would be able to hear what he said. 'Sometimes,' he whispered, 'it is necessary to sacrifice love, too.'

He let go of me and stood back. Someone came to stand in front of me. I could tell that he had the log book in his hand.

'You must sign,' Bissolati said simply.

'Otto?'

'It is your right,' Otto said.

'And your duty,' Max called. There was another click. He had been taking photographs all the time. 'There is plenty of space below my signature and Hansi's,' he said.

'Give me the pencil,' I said.

I could not grip the pencil and it tumbled down among the dismantled stones. Someone retrieved it and sharpened it with a knife, and then it was fitted as tightly as possible into my hand.

'I'll steady your arm,' Otto said.

Bissolati held the book, Otto steadied my arm, and I scrawled an approximation of my signature. All the time I could hear the shutter of Max's camera.

'You must say about Hansi,' Max said.

'It would be the honourable thing to do,' Otto agreed.

I nodded, and after a few seconds I could hear him write down some words. 'What have you said?' I asked.

He read it aloud. 'This is the signature of Ernst Tinnion, from England, who made the first direct ascent of the Versücherin north wall with his friend Hansi Kirchner, who died that he might succeed.'

'That's good,' Max said, taking another photograph.

'Put the date down,' Bissolati said.

Max walked across to me. 'Don't look so gloomy, Ernst; today you have become a hero.'

He and Bissolati added their names as witnesses, the date was written in the margin, the log closed. It was placed back in its case, the tiny couplings fastened, and the leather belt tightened around it. Then the case was lowered into its recess and the stones stacked around it until, at last, it was covered again.

I stood in front of the cairn with my head bowed, the rope hanging from my chest.

'Herr Tinnion,' Otto said gently, 'it is time we left the mountain.'

7

IT TOOK AN AGE TO DESCEND THE EAST RIDGE. WHEN WE BEGAN, THE afternoon sun had already cast much of our path into shadow, and I was told that the ice was slippery even though the route was well marked. Otto was determined to be first down into the valley so that he could spread the news. He bade me a gruffly emotional goodbye and went on ahead. I was left with Max, Bissolati and the five other members of the Italian team.

They carried me on a stretcher. It was no more than a canvas sling carried between two poles. Leather belts had been passed through the metal eyelets in the canvas, and these were tightened and buckled so that I could move very little. I was transported down the mountain like a patient from an operation, and as we moved the canvas creaked as if it was a sail in a strong wind.

My bearers picked their way as carefully as possible, but the descent was uncomfortable and sometimes painful. On several occasions I had to be put down onto the ice and then slid down a gradient. Some would secure ropes to the stretcher and lower me; others would steer my descent. Often one of my escort would speak to me in friendly, encouraging Italian, as if they were proud and honoured to have saved my life. They knew I did not understand, but must have realised that the sound of voices would give me reassurance. None of them spoke either German or English, apart from Bissolati; all of them tried to use a few basic vernacular phrases, as if they would comfort me.

For some time I lost consciousness. Oblivion came upon me suddenly, and without warning, and then the movement of the stretcher jerked me awake again. Sometimes, too, a dream or

141

hallucination filled my mind with a vividly realised image of the summit. Hansi and I stood unharmed and alone beside the cairn, our faces glowing with brotherhood and triumph. We looked like teenage boys, and when Hansi shook my hand there was no trace of gangrene, and his hand was whole. All the time, though, I could hear the rough, irregular rhythms of my descent on the stretcher.

After this I came to believe that the sky had darkened, although my vision was so dim that I could not be sure. 'Bissolati?' I asked.

But it was Max who answered me. 'How do you feel?' he asked.

'Is it night? Or is this a storm?'

'Do not worry; it is only night which has fallen. Are you in pain?'

I could not answer him. He repeated the question.

'At times,' I said.

'Is it bad?'

'No.'

'We are going as quickly as we can. Before long those straps can be loosened. We're almost at the hut.'

For a few delirious seconds I thought he meant the abandoned farm. It must have showed in my face.

'No, Ernst,' Max said, 'we mean the old military hut just below the col. We will have to spend the night there.'

I wanted to be off the mountain. 'Bissolati?' I asked, wanting to plead with him.

Max continued. 'I've been examining your hands. I'm not an expert, of course, but I have seen worse. I do not think you will lose your fingers. As regards your blindness, that too will be no hardship. A few weeks under bandages, then gauze, and your sight will be as good as new.'

'And my face?'

'Rest and warmth will cure you of much. Your eyebrows have been burned away. An accident with a heater?'

'I was too close to lightning. And I drank raw alcohol. I had to, otherwise I would have died.'

'I can still smell it from your coat,' Bissolati said. 'Are you haemorrhaging, do you think?'

'I could taste blood, but I can't now.'

'The veins in your face have broken,' Max said.

I thought of my youth, vanquished by the wall, and of the strange face, tattooed with ruptured bloodvessels, that would gaze back at me from a mirror.

'Max,' I said.

'Yes?'

'Hansi told me about the job. He would never have taken it.'

Bissolati spoke before Max could reply. 'We will have to rest here for ten, twenty minutes,' he said. 'The next section will be difficult with the stretcher. We need to cut holds in the ice. Max, it will be done more quickly if the six of us do this. Will you stay with our friend here?'

Max agreed, and I was rested on a table of smooth rock while the Italians went forward. I could hear them talking for a while, and then their voices faded.

I could detect Max's presence at my side, even though he did not speak for several minutes. Finally he said, 'You misjudge your friend.'

'Hansi wasn't interested in politics. Especially not in your kind of politics.'

'*My* kind? How do you know what that is?'

'Don't try to be innocent, Max. You know exactly what I mean.'

'You think, perhaps, that he faked an interest in the German methods of education? He seemed genuine to me. Eager, even.'

I did not reply.

'In a way, you are right,' Max said grudgingly. 'Hansi was a simple soul, and I did not want him for his politics. I wanted him for his reputation, and for his glamour. He would have been given what he wanted. In return, he would have done what he was asked to do. Including, in due course, swearing allegiance to another flag.'

'He wasn't so malleable.'

'Don't lie, Ernst. We both know that he was ill at ease with the realities of everyday life. So much so that a clever person could twist him round their little finger. He would have had no trouble with our political requirements, because he was so naïve. He was a man who needed to put his faith into something, so he put it into simple things – into friendship, and into mountaineering. In the end it was a friend, and a mountain, that killed him.'

If I twisted my head I could see Max's shape, featureless and monolithic, as it rose above me.

'It is a great pity,' he went on; 'he was just what we wanted – a man of both achievement and potential.' He paused, then spoke again. 'You would not do at all, I'm afraid. He could have taught team spirit better than you. What is more, he would have believed in it.'

'I wouldn't want your job, Max.'

'No?'

'No. I prefer to sort out my own future. Besides, I don't believe a word of what gets taught in those places. And apart from anything else I'm the wrong nationality, thank God.'

He clicked his tongue. 'I did not suspect you of being so British. Do you hate foreigners so much?'

'You know that isn't true. You used to have a civilised, enlightened country, Max. What happened to it?'

'We had a corrupt, frightened one. It was somewhat like yours, Ernest – the people were poorly educated, unfit, out of work, without pride. All that has changed.'

'You're a party man through and through, aren't you?'

'Not so. You accuse me of holding beliefs which I do not hold. You forget that I am a much-travelled, experienced, and cultivated man. I am neither narrow-minded nor petty. And I owe no allegiance to party politics.'

'You would do whatever they wanted you to do. Don't lie.'

He bent and whispered in my ear, as if confessing a secret. 'Not so. I am an artist; an artist with a camera. I know exactly what my responsibilities are.'

'Like Leni Riefenstahl, you mean.'

'Of course. I met her in Berlin; she has filmed a masterpiece. There is no doubt about it. I can say that even though it will be a long time before we see the film.'

'By the time she finishes cutting it, the Olympics will have been forgotten.'

'She filmed the Nuremberg rallies. Who has forgotten those? Once they have seen her film, who *can* forget? It will be the same with the Olympics. Even you must recognise that she under-stands, Ernst. Didn't you and Hansi go to see one of her films a long time ago?'

I tried to lick my lips, but could not. 'Yes. It was a climbing film. We thought she was wonderful.'

I could hear him chuckle. 'And, of course, she was. I have seen some of those films myself. They appeal to an unsophisticated audience, but that is to be welcomed. Often the simple, the naïve can see problems more clearly than those who have spent their lives studying them. The people now in government in Germany are such people; they can see problems and they can sweep them away. It is like a great purification, a great surge of confidence which is spreading outwards from its centre, and which will eventually restore the health and vitality of all Europe, and then beyond. Leni and I can see beyond the immediate and the mundane. In sport, in human struggle, we can see the promise of glory. You were not at Berlin, Ernst. You should have been. You would have been able to see a new nobility take shape.'

'And that's what you serve?'

'See the film, study my photographs, and perhaps you will be able to understand better than you do now. You could tell me that some of our leaders are small, petty men; I can tell you that, even in them, there is something at work which is greater than us and which will last longer than we can comprehend. That is the way of evolution. The clever, the fit, the decisive will inherit the earth.'

'You're crazy and you're evil,' I said.

'And you, my friend, and Hansi Kirchner as well, and the Seematters, and the woman who has masqueraded as your wife, you are all innocents who cannot recognise the world around you. You are insular, blinkered. Like children at play, you have organised your games of sport, of false marriage, of pretend friendship. I have seen through you all the time.'

'Hansi told you we weren't married. You didn't find out yourself.'

'As soon as I met you and Jean I could detect a falseness about you. You did not have the self-centred foolishness of honeymooners. There was a shiftiness about you, and an uneasiness about her.'

'This has nothing to do with you. Isn't Bissolati back yet?'

'Its consequences have.'

'Do you have to interfere in all of our lives, Max? Even the rescue party would have been better off without you.'

'I would not let them go without me. I needed those photographs.' He was silent for several seconds, then went on. 'I was impressed by Jean. Even Bruno sensed that she has a talent which you do not have, and perhaps never could have.'

'A talent for getting on with people, you mean? What does that matter?'

'Because of what happened to his parents, Bruno is very suspicious. And yet he and Jean have become very close. She has been looking after him since you began your climb. I would not like their friendship to be ended.'

'So?'

'Ernst, even to you it must be obvious that Jean has no future if she stays with you.'

'What?'

'No man will be able to keep her happy. Not yet. You should recognise that. *She* recognises it.'

'You're a fool. We love each other.'

'Of course you do. But what about happiness, fulfilment, a future? Love has nothing to do with such things.'

'It means more than any of them.'

'Can you really believe what your poets have told you? Jean, too, has read much of that kind of thing.'

'You must have talked to her a lot,' I said, with as much irony poured into my words as I could summon.

His reply was matter-of-fact. 'Yes, when you were on the wall. But do not think of accusing her. She would never betray you.'

'What gives you the right to speak to me like this?' I asked with a sudden fury.

He did not answer, and I thought that my question had shamed him.

'Well?' I demanded, thinking that he might not dare to reply.

'Because everything has changed,' he said. 'I saw the solution days ago. Now, she too sees the wisdom of it. Soon, I shall be her employer.'

I was stunned. 'Employer?' I repeated, idiotically.

'It is logical when you think about it. For much of the year I am away from home because of my work. My mother is growing old. Jean will be perfect for Bruno. I want you to realise that this is purely a business arrangement that I have suggested; Jean would have her own room at the top of the house. After a few years she will be free to do what she wants. Of course, there will be difficulties taking her into the country – but I know enough people to have those smoothed over.'

'Why are you doing this? Can't you stop this compulsion to rearrange other people's lives? Be a photographer, Max. Do what you like, but don't involve yourself with Jean or with me.'

'But I have responsiblities. We all have. I cannot let Jean ruin herself over you. And I am the only one who can give her a breathing space. You follow a hazardous course, Ernest. She may have told you that she wanted to spend her life with you, but you are not a good prospect for a woman like Jean.'

'I was all she wanted.'

'No. She wanted your sense of adventure, but she did not realise that you would force it to extremes. She wanted you for your European qualities, but now she must see that you are little more than a mere tourist. Most of all you were a means of escape.'

'I was far more than that. I *am* more than that.'

'You are a man overtaken by the revolution he had helped to create. You have been left behind by the speed of events. Jean is a free woman who must be rational about her future. She needs challenge, not danger. And she needs newness, but she must have stability. And I can see that, most of all, she wishes to learn.'

'Learn? Learn what? She's given up everything she set out to learn.'

'Unlike you, she thinks about the future, and wishes to learn about it. And where is that future being created? Not in the mill towns of England, but here in the heart of Europe. She has come to me because she instinctively understands this. In return for a few pleasant duties she will get food, shelter, even friends. She will have a chance to become a different person.'

'You talk as if everything is already arranged. You may not have as much power as you think, Max.'

'Oh, I don't think there is any doubt about what will happen. She is a woman of resilience and courage.'

'And what does she have to believe in?' I asked bitterly. 'The same things Hansi would have had to swear to? That's the only way she'll be able to stay in your country.'

Max laughed. 'Come, Ernst, admit it is an admirable scheme. In your heart of hearts you may even approve it, because it lets you off the hook with her, yes? It is no devil's pact.' Now he spoke to me with the easy familiarity of a brother. 'No woman in her right mind would want to stay with you. Women needs families around them – their own or someone else's. What did you leave Jean with? The promise to return from the wall? That's not very much. I would not be surprised if you secretly wished to be rid of her. You're a selfish man, but you're a man of action. And Jean must know what Otto knows, and I know, and every member of this team knows.'

I said nothing, but felt weakness run through me like crystals turned suddenly to water.

'Hansi Kirchner,' Max whispered, 'was alive when you cut the rope.'

My heart slowed; I felt it. 'That's not true,' I said in a broken voice.

'Oh, we all know that this must not be admitted. Never. We know that you must deny it, as *we* would deny it.'

'Hansi had been dead for hours,' I said. I could not understand why my voice sounded like a liar's.

'No one blames you. You did what was necessary to save the attempt from utter failure. I salute you for your deed, if not for your honesty. You will be called a hero for this climb. The real hero was the man who hung at the bottom of that rope.'

Because of the way I had been lashed onto the stretcher I could only move my head a little way, and yet I tried to shake it. 'I swear to you I didn't even try to cut the rope when he was alive,' I said.

'You are a man after my own heart, Ernst. You, too, know that the end must justify the means. Otherwise you would still be on that wall, frozen to Hansi Kirchner. *He* would never have cut the rope, because climbing was at his heart, but friendship was his soul. Do not worry; your secret is safe with us.'

'It didn't happen like that,' I said in desperation, and struggled within my harness, but I had to fall back.

He put his hand to my forehead, like a doctor. 'Calm yourself; you must rest.' Then he added, as if consoling me; 'We must preserve the myth, whatever happens. People steer their lives by events such as this, even if they are lies. The truth hardly matters.'

'Truth? You're a photographer. Don't you care about truth?'

'I care about a higher truth. I depict men as if they are divine. I must find transcendence even in the squalid and the mundane. A great sculptor may be given a slab of rough marble and see within it the form of his masterpiece. I am given a stream of images, and within them I must search for, and find, those which can be fixed to show elation, grief, pain.'

'You wanted me to be like that, didn't you?'

'But you are like that. When we found you on the icefield you looked truly remarkable. You were a man who had been savagely beaten, and yet who refused to lie down. I took a lot of photographs of you. All the time I was aware that I would never be given such a chance again. I shall be careful about my selection of them – scrupulous, even. The images will exalt you, and your expression, your stance on the ice will be an inspiration to others. Why, just by looking at you men will gain insight and determination.'

'What will they see, Max? A pair of blinded eyes? A face made ugly by the struggle? That would be no picture of triumph.'

'Of course they will be. Why pretend otherwise? The whole climb has been vivid, engrossing, dramatic – a friendship tested to breaking point, victory wrestled from the very jaws of failure, and, in the end, the conquest of a north wall which everyone said was unclimbable. If you had been German, Ernst, you would have got that Olympic medal.'

'I would have refused it.'

'Liar. You would have relished it. Why not? You would have deserved it. You have survived the most terrible ordeal amongst the worst high-level storms that anyone can ever remember. You can never turn your back on this achievement; your face is branded by it. Why, the mountain itself is seen as something extraordinary. All mountains are; that is why our ancestors

150

believed that gods lived on their summits. That's why you, and millions of others, flocked to see the films that Leni made when she was an actress. You recognised that she was the priestess of a cult, the object of a million dreams. The mountains were pure, and they were deadly. They promised hardship and death, but they also gave her glamour, romance, mystery. Consciously or not, her audience understood the potency, the symbolism. They recognised the thrill of ice.'

I could hear the sound of Bissolati and his men returning. If I turned my head as far as it would go I thought I could see their lanterns shining like ghost-lights in the gloom, but I was aware that my vision was fading rapidly.

'It's not like that,' I said. My voice was hollow when I spoke.

Max lowered his voice further as the Italians approached. 'Whether you want it or not,' he whispered, 'you are condemned to be a hero. My work will make your face and your achievement known across the generations. In fifty years time, a hundred, people will point to *your* image on *my* photograph and say that *this* was the man who first scaled the Versücherin wall. You will be a testament to the spirit of man, struggling against the odds; I shall have given you immortality. We are bound together, you and I. But you can never cut me free.'

Bissolati's team approached us, the ice crunching beneath their boots. Soon I could hear him begin to explain how I would be lowered down the last sheer slope before the hut.

I scarcely heard him, and I hardly felt the jolts, the slides, the giddying sway as I was transported down the last swell of the east ridge. My mind felt as if it had been emptied. I had lost everything.

The team stopped before the hut, laid me on the ground, and unbuckled the straps that bound me. I was carried through the door and propped up against a wall. I could see nothing. Then the others sat beside me. The hut was small, and there was no space for anyone to lie down, so we sat like polar explorers waiting for a storm to pass. We were shoulder to shoulder, and our legs crossed each other's. One or two smoked, and someone talked in a low, pleasant voice throughout most of the night. The man next to me even fell asleep; I could hear his deep, relaxed breathing. Several times Max, or Bissolati, asked me gently if I was all right. I said that I was.

When I was not awake I drifted between sleep and delirium. During the night, when all else was quiet, I heard Hansi scratch at the hut door with his butchered hand. I shouted aloud with fear, but was calmed as if I was a frightened child. It was only the mice, I was told, gnawing at the wood behind our backs.

Later, Otto told me that people came for miles to see our descent of the mountain. I was in a blur of exhaustion and pain, and often did not recognise what was happening. I scarcely knew where I was, and lay within a fog of noise and movement, not realising that pilgrims had gathered around the rescue party as it made its way down the last stages. When the boots were razored from my feet I mistook the release for anguish, and shouted out loud.

I recognised Jean's voice when I heard it, but I had no way of knowing that I had been set down in a harvested field, and that her legs were flecked with blood because she had come running through the stubble. A doctor was examining me and telling someone about my condition, but his comments did not even seem to be about me, and I thought he was describing another climber.

I tried to raise myself, but could not. I began to speak Jean's name, over and over again, and it was a minute or so before I realised that she was beside me. She must have come to see me then walked away, but been drawn back by my reiteration of her name.

'Jean,' I said, 'don't just leave.'

'No,' she said, 'no.'

I was carried down to the valley floor. Someone had arranged for an ambulance to take me straight to a hospital ten miles away. When I protested I was told that the doctor insisted. I shouted for Otto, whose voice responded from only a short distance. 'Otto,' I said, 'ten minutes, that's all.'

'I understand,' he said.

While the ambulancemen waited, cursing my stupidity, and hundreds of watchers gathered round the door, I was stretched out in the Seematters' dining room and the doors were closed. Jean was the only other person in the room.

I wanted to tell her how much she had meant to me, but instead I was filled with humiliation and anger.

'You're leaving with Max Volkwein,' I said bitterly.

I could see nothing, and did not know what she was wearing, or what the expression was on her face. I could only smell her perfume, and feel the light touch of her fingers as she wiped my face.

At first she did not reply.

'Well?'

'I have no choice,' she said. I felt her hand under my head as she lifted me slightly. A cloth that smelled of disinfectant was rubbed slowly across my cheeks.

'Choice,' I repeated, sneering the word.

'Don't you understand, Ernest?'

'I understand that I've been used, that's all.'

'That's not true.'

'No? How would *you* put it?'

'Ernest, it *has* been my fault, I see that now. But I never thought of it as using you. And I realise that you must blame me, and that you must be terribly, terribly hurt. But try to see things from my point of view.'

'You made no attempt to see them from mine.'

'I've spent a long time doing just that.'

I tried to snort, but could not.

'Close your lips,' she said gently. I obeyed, and felt the cloth swab me. 'I tried to ignore realities,' she went on. 'I sincerely believed that events would take a new course, and that all the difficulties would resolve themselves and somehow go away. But when we went to the glacier – well, then I knew that I would have to do *something*.'

'You said nothing to me.'

'Ernest, it must have been obvious to you. What had happened to Hansi just a few weeks ago? He'd watched one of the best climbers of his generation die just a few feet from safety. Did you expect me to be untroubled by that? It brought it home to me when I met him. You both seemed to have so little chance.'

'You wanted to be part of our adventure, Jean. You always said so.'

'I didn't know what the Versücherin would be really like. I had no conception of snowblindness, frostbite, or the kind of death that Hansi had. I wanted the thrill of it; I wanted the romance.'

'The kind you get from Max's photographs, you mean?'

'There's no danger in what Max does, Ernest. He won't ever be faced with the kind of problem you had – and please, I don't want to hear the details of how Hansi died. I just want to be with someone who'll never have to do what you did.'

'Max climbs, Jean.'

'He climbs the easy trails, just as he indulges himself in sports that aren't truly demanding or dangerous. I think that's a wise course to take.'

'He's a schemer, Jean. He connives. He distorts. He'll do anything to further a political end.'

'Max isn't political. Not really. In many ways you and he are the same.'

'That's a lie. I could never think that.'

'Why not? You each have dreamy, unreal notions of how people should live. Grand schemes, master-plans, absurd theories. You both believe in a kind of *perfection*. And you both

154

think that something has been proved by the simple act of climbing a high, dangerous mountain. It hasn't. You haven't added a grain to the sum total of human happiness, and you haven't subtracted from it either. It's a pointless sport, performed for its own sake. You make no difference at all to the state of the world.' She paused. I knew she was studying my face, and I was pleased that I could not see her expression.

'And you,' I asked, 'what do *you* do? Compromise? Settle for second best – or worse?'

'Of course. I'm like most people. I survive, and try to make things better for myself. I look for chances, and weigh up whether or not I should take them. I have to compromise because I can't live my life if I don't.'

'You'll never be able to work for Max Volkwein. You're walking into a trap.'

'Ernest, he really *is* like you. Neither of you will ever be truly satisfied, because you both want humanity to be more than it can be. Look at his photographs – they're too arranged, too formal. He makes people look like pieces of sculpture.'

'They're not just that. They stand for things. Things they may not realise.'

'He used roll after roll of film on you, Ernest. He'd taken plenty before you began, but he must have taken lots more just on the summit. He's worried about the cold having damaged some of the equipment, too. He wants to take all the films back to Munich to have them developed under the best conditions.' She paused, and I heard her strike a match. She had started to smoke again. 'That's why he wants to leave straight away,' she added.

After a few more seconds, I asked, 'Straight away?'

There was a catch in her voice. 'Otto told me they were all caught in the storm on the east ridge. Max will be worried about that, too. Damp could have got into the cameras.'

'Jean, I hope all his photographs have been ruined. Every one.'

'You can't mean that.'

'Even the ones he took before we began. I'm serious.'

'They'll be all right. I know they will.'

'If they are, then I don't want to see them. Ever.'

'They'll make you world-famous. Won't that help?'

'They're too high a price to pay.'

She was silent. Someone tapped on the door. 'They're telling us that it's time for you to leave,' Jean said.

'I'm never going to climb again,' I said.

She was silent.

'I've made up my mind.' I spoke as firmly as I could.

'Ernest, that can't change things now. You've made that decision far too late.'

'Hansi said that, if it would help things, he would never climb again. But he decided that if he never set foot on another mountain he would not save another climber's life. He was wrong. Now it's my turn to decide.'

There was another knock on the door.

'I don't want to be an example to anyone,' I went on. 'If I can do nothing about the photographs, then the least I can do is turn my back on their effects.'

'Poor Ernest,' she said, 'you live in such a simple world. What will you do?'

'I don't know. After I've recovered, I'm going home, back to England. I used to think that I belonged here. I can't believe that now.'

'Max says the future is being made a long way away from England.'

'And Bissolati thinks the future will be a war. And you'll be in the middle of it.'

She gripped my shoulder. 'Don't worry; Max is certain that there won't be a war. Even if there is, I have a good protector.'

This time the knock was more insistent.

'Ernest,' she said, 'you must go now. It's for your own good. I

156

wish you all the luck in the world. Will you do the same for me? Despite everything?'

I tried to nod. 'Yes,' I said.

She kissed me lightly on the cheek, so lightly that I could scarcely detect her touch.

'Ernest,' she whispered, 'I love you. You may not realise that, but I do.'

'Yes?' I asked, bitterly, and the door was opened. I heard Jean stand up suddenly, and then there was nothing but the sound of boots on the Seematters' floor. I was lifted up by strong hands to be carried outside. Everyone was talking; there was a riot of German, Italian, English. My mouth felt as if it was full of blood, and although I tried to speak Jean's name, I could not.

They were the last moments we ever had together.

My bed was comfortable, the sheets crisply laundered, and the flowers on my windowledge filled the room with their scent. For several days my eyes remained bandaged. At first I had difficulty detecting even the filament of a light when it was shone directly into my pupils, but then, after the gauze was peeled off some days later, I could make out a wall, the door, and a rectangle of sky through the window. I could always listen to the noises from outside my room – the shuffling of other patients, or the squeak of the rubber-ringed wheels on the trolleys.

My hands and toes were bandaged, too, and were unwrapped for examination three times a day. Each time I was told how well I was progressing, and that I was a very fortunate man.

Reporters were forbidden to see me, but I was allowed friends. At my request, Otto issued a statement about our ascent of the north wall. He gave details of our route, reminded everyone that Hansi and I had been friends since boyhood, and stated that I owed my life to him. He also stressed that Hansi had been dead for several hours before I cut the rope.

Four days after I was admitted to the hospital the Versücherin north wall was climbed again. Bissolati and his team did it. Afterwards he came to see me. They had followed the route that Hansi had planned, and had perfect weather all the way. Although they looked for Hansi's body, they saw no sign of it.

Otto and Clara insisted on taking care of me as soon as I left the hospital. They did this without payment, and forever refused my attempts to make some sort of recompense. They nursed me out of simple goodness and pride, and said nothing to disturb my long silences. Gradually, my vision returned.

Otto requested only one thing; that he be allowed to keep my boots. I laughed and agreed, not knowing why he should want them. 'Because they are part of history,' he said, and showed them to me. The strips of leather hung from them like gigantic fringes. They looked like carnival boots.

I had already asked Otto to write to my parents, for I would have to stay with them on my return to England. When I received a letter I thought it must be from them, but then I saw the Hitler stamp on the envelope. Jean had written to me.

She had her own room at the top of the Volkwein house. Max's mother was a delightful lady, and Jean and Bruno had become the best of friends. Everywhere she went the people were so friendly, and full of such confidence. There was little doubt that she had taken the right decision. Max was away on an assignment, but would be back soon. He had to visit the authorities a lot to make sure Jean was classed as an official resident in the country. She said she hoped my recovery was now complete, but she made no mention of our parting, or of Max's photographs of me. At the close, she asked me to let Harry know that, in the end, everything was working out for the best. And she signed her letter with the word *love*.

I thought about the letter for a long time. Perhaps Bissolati, ascending the wall so soon after me, had taken the immediacy from Max's photographs. Nevertheless I was surprised that neither I, nor the Seematters, had ever seen any.

Shortly after this I told Otto and Clara the truth about Jean and me. Neither of them was surprised, but Clara said that she still thought that it had been a tragic way for any relationship to end.

Just before I left the valley a man came to whitewash over the mural on the front of the pension. When the hunting scene was obliterated, and the wash had dried, he began to paint two climbers ascending the north wall of the Versücherin. Their faces had the flatness of icons, and they ascended an impossible precipice roped together as if nothing could ever part them.

It was almost three years before I heard from Jean again. She wrote directly to me, having obtained my address from the Seematters. By then I was living quietly in a town near the Pennines. I had begun to climb again, but always on British cliffs, and never on severe ones. I had lost much of my vigour and some of my nerve, and never told anyone that I had been the first man up the Versücherin north face.

Harry had divorced Jean. She had not contested the suit, for she needed to marry Max quickly. She wanted me to appreciate that this was a sensible course of action, for then she would become a German citizen, protected by the laws of her adopted country. Everyone was sure there would be no war, for the British were far too sensible to let such a thing happen. Although she did not say it, I could read between the lines that there must have already been some unpleasant scenes around her.

In the years that followed, I often thought about Jean and Max. I wondered if Max was doing war work, and if he perhaps had photographed the very pilots who had flown in formation across my parents' house on their way to bomb Jean's home country. I wondered what Bruno would do, with his obsessions and his dependence on kindness. Most of all I thought about Jean, and about the kind of life she must be leading in a country which had now become our bitter enemy. I even wrote to the Seematters to see if they had heard anything, but they had not.

Towards the end of the war they passed on to me a letter written by Max. It arrived on a sunny, bright morning. There was a summer warmth in the air, and it seemed that we were entering a hopeful, just future.

Jean was dead. She had been killed in an air-raid. A bomb had sliced straight through the roof of the house and exploded it from the inside. When Max and Bruno had returned they had found a pile of bricks, a broken water-main, and a solitary high roof-beam which burned steadily. Fragments of charred paper had been blown down the street, and the gutters were full of shrivelled twists of negative.

Jean had been in the house with Max's mother. Among the rubble there were splashes of blood and scorched pieces of dress. Apart from that, no trace of them was ever found.

Two years later, during the first post-war attempt on the north wall, a Swiss team found Hansi's body while they were pioneer-ing a new route. He lay within a jumble of rocks near the base of the flume. Cold had desiccated his body so that it had become grey and fragile, like that of a mummy.

He was buried in a tiny church in the valley. I sent a letter of sympathy, but did not attend.

8

IT WAS FIFTY YEARS BEFORE WE MADE OUR PEACE. NO ONE RECOGnised me when I walked across the town square, even though flags were to fly in my honour. To the workmen stringing bunting across the street I was just another old man, white-haired and a little uncertain. But I was to be at the centre of nostalgia and ceremony. There would be reporters to ask me questions, and photographers to follow me on a helicopter ride up the mountain.

The weather was as hot and as still as it had been when Jean and I first arrived in the valley, and the statue of the armoured horseman still stood in the town square, although tiny bright flags radiated from him in six different directions. When I looked round I could see that most of the old shops had gone, and that now they sold pizzas and cola drinks and souvenir cuckoo clocks. The old camera shop had become twice its original size, and behind its plate-glass window there were automatic and video cameras stacked on plastic stands. There were climbers' shops, too, which sold multicoloured nylon rope, safety helmets in bright primary colours, waterproof clothing that weighed only a few ounces, and high-protein food condensed into tiny cans. In the windows were credit-card stickers, and a range of envelopes posted from all parts of the mountainous world – Chile, Nepal, New Zealand.

All the time it seemed that fate had played a callous trick on me, for the memories rose, vivid and startling, through the everyday life of the valley. It was easy to forget half a century and believe that the Seematters still lived, that Bissolati and most of his friends had not been killed with the partisans, and that the future was still alive with possibilities. I could recall everyone exactly as they had been all those years ago – Otto with his smirk of pride, Jean with her sensuality and her laugh, Hansi as he embraced me within the confines of his tent.

I remembered meeting Max and Bruno as if it had only been a week ago when they had walked from the camera shop. I still thought of Max as looking as he had in his early thirties, with that lopsided cast to his face because of his broken nose, and in my mind Bruno was forever young and forever surly, with the unattractiveness of the obsessed.

I walked into a hotel that had been built a short way down from the main square, and there they were.

At first I did not recognise them. Max was a frail pensioner with a bald head, dark glasses, and a cane. Bruno was a prosperous grey-haired man with a moustache, who looked as if he was about to enjoy a long, healthy retirement. I was shocked to think that they saw age, and perhaps also death, in me.

They shook my hands as if we were old friends, and as if no ill feeling had ever passed between us. I told Max that I had once read an interview with him; it had been ten years ago, I said. He surprised me by telling me it had been eighteen years. Some recent photographs had been printed in one of the colour supplements. Max had visited a Sudanese tribe for several seasons, and an exhibition of his work had been organised. The tribe wore few, if any, clothes and was distinguised by a tall, feline athleticism which occasionally moved into ritualised, brutal violence. I had immediately thought of his photographs from Berlin.

'I shall go back to Sudan, too,' Max said. 'As soon as I get better.'

He leaned forward, one hand spread across the head of his cane. Behind the tinted lenses his eyes looked pale, and there were blotches across his scalp. He was much thinner than he had been, and his nose had become hawkish, so that he looked both weakened and sinister.

'It may be my last goodbye,' he said.

'Uncle has been unwell,' Bruno explained. 'He wishes to visit all his favourite places before it is too late. I keep telling him not to be such a pessimist. He is a healthy man for his age.'

Bruno spoke with a detectable American accent. It overlaid his natural German so heavily that its outline was barely discernible. He had the air of a successful professional man – a lawyer, perhaps, or a doctor.

'I am pleased that you heard about me,' Max went on. 'I read many of the climbing magazines after we parted, Ernst, but I heard nothing about you at all. I have only read of you in connection with the north wall. What other climbing did you do?'

I looked out of the hotel window. Flowers had been placed on the ledge in a vase, but if I looked past them I could see bandsmen walking towards the square. In an hour the anniversary celebrations would begin.

'I gave it up,' I said.

'Because of your injuries?'

'Because my heart was no longer in it.'

'I am sorry.'

'You needn't be. And you, Bruno – what about you?'

Bruno smiled in a way which he must have thought was modest. 'I had good fortune. I am a dentist now. In America.'

'You surprise me. I thought your future was with animals.'

He shrugged. 'It was a boy's enthusiasm, nothing more.'

I wondered what he had done in the war, but did not ask. He would have lied to me anyway.

'I went back into teaching,' I said.

'Ah,' Max said, without irony, 'so you are not a poet.'

'No,' I replied, 'I'm not a poet.' I was nothing very much. The only thing I had been was the first man to climb the Versücherin north wall.

We sat for several seconds without speaking. The years darkened between us.

'She was happy with us, Ernst,' Max said suddenly. I looked sharply at him and he nodded sagely, as if he would only be contradicted by a fool. 'It's true,' he added quietly.

'If she hadn't gone with you she might still be alive.'

'Perhaps. But many of us could make accusations like that. And besides, it was *your* people who killed her.' He smiled colourlessly. 'It was more than forty years ago. We have all lived full lives since then.'

'Yes,' I said, without expression.

'We found nothing of either Jean or my mother. Not straight away.'

I looked at him, not certain of what he was trying to say. Bruno linked his hands together and looked down at them. 'What do you mean, Max?' I asked.

'Many years later the house opposite us was being rebuilt. It had survived the bomb virtually intact – it had lost a few tiles, nothing more. But when it had to have a new roof on, they found something wedged between the tiles and the roofbeams. It was an arm. It was complete from elbow to finger.'

I felt a shiver run through me like a fear, and my mouth went dry. 'Hers?' I asked.

'It must have been flung there by the blast,' Bruno explained. 'Once lodged there, in dry conditions, the flesh would have . . .' His voice tailed away.

'We knew it was Jean's by the ring,' Max said. 'When the arm was lifted free, the ring fell from her finger and landed in the street.'

I nodded.

'We had it cremated. The ring was put back on her finger. It seemed appropriate. I hope you do not object.'

'Why should I? It has nothing to do with me.'

'But it was not her wedding-ring; that had vanished. No, it was the ring you gave her, which she always insisted on wearing on another finger. It had lost its golden colour, but it made no difference to her.'

'You let her keep that ring?'

'Of course it was an embarrassment because it was so cheap. But I gave in to her, as I gave in to her on many other things.' He regarded me with a cool, watery gaze. 'She thought about you a lot, Ernst, but she never regretted doing what she did. She knew how to take decisions when they became necessary, and she could see her way through a series of problems. I admired her for that. Although she persuaded me, at times, to do things which I know to have been wrong.'

'I didn't think you were ever capable of being persuaded.'

'I'm like all men; a fool for a pretty woman. She persuaded me not to publish your photographs. Did you know that?'

I shook my head. 'No,' I said. My ribs felt light and fragile as a bird's.

'She gave me many reasons. None of them were very good, and I knew that all she wanted was to protect you from any further distress. So, to keep her happy, I stored them.'

'They were good?'

'Some of them were my best work. Placing, texture, tone, expression were all perfect. I want you to realise that I did it for her, and for her alone. I wanted her to be happy. And what were a few photographs to me, anyway? I had already made my mark, and would make it again.'

'You still have them, then.'

He looked at me in silence for a few moments. 'When the bomb hit my house, the sky must have been filled by burning pieces of paper, and my negatives withered as if a blow-torch had passed across them. Within a split-second, most of my past vanished. And, Ernst, your past vanished as well.'

I should have been relieved. Instead I found that I was disappointed. More than half a lifetime had passed since those photographs had been taken. I wondered if the passage of time would have cleansed them of all politics, all heroism, and made them nothing but images fixed on paper. I felt a sudden wave of regret flood me, then ebb. It was as if I had lost something precious, and yet had only just realised its value.

'I'm glad,' I said. Across all the years, I still wanted revenge, no matter how small, for all the injuries Max had given me.

'Our losses were tiny parts of a wider tragedy,' he said as if to placate me.

'Perhaps it was fortunate for you that it happened, Max. You were a supporter of the Reich, and a propagandist for it. Having the evidence destroyed must have been the best thing that could have happened to you. You could claim to be an innocent civilian. Both of you could.'

Bruno looked at me with a sad, betrayed expression. 'That's really unfair, Mr Tinnion,' he said.

'Ernst,' Max said calmly, 'fifty years have not changed you. You still wish to accuse others. Have you learned no wisdom?'

'You don't fool me, Max. You never have done. You've just adapted to change, that's all.'

'And you are the one who has held out against it, always?'

'Something like that,' I said with a grim satisfaction.

He gave a small, unhealthy sigh. 'I had hoped that we would meet as friends,' he said, 'but now I see that is not possible. We are too old for arguments, though. What do you think that people want to see at this celebration? Certainly not peevish old men, still sniping at each other across the years. No; they want us to be venerable, wise, united by memory and achievement.'

'*My* achievement.'

'You would have died without others, Ernst. You should not allow yourself to forget that. Come, it is the anniversary. Let us be united, just for those who have come to see us.'

'You always knew what the public wanted.'

'Everyone knows what the public wants – food, shelter, other people. Beyond that, they want heroes. Let us make amends, Ernst. You and I are the only ones left.'

He extended a hand. I hesitated, and he withdrew it.

Bruno made a clicking noise of disapproval, and shook his head. 'This is ridiculous,' he said.

'You need not fear me,' Max continued. 'I have your best interests at heart. Looking back, you should be able to see that has always been true. But we must make peace with our memories. Is that not why you are here?'

I nodded reluctantly.

'We *must* be friends. The world has left us both behind. What are we now but spent men, whose lives are nearing their end? Let us show that we once shared something special, something historic.'

Once more he stretched out his hand. This time I took it, and he placed the palm of his other hand across my knuckles. I suppressed a shiver.

'Good,' he said gently, 'good.'

I felt like an animal that has been coaxed into performing a trick.

Bruno leaned forward and clasped me by the shoulder. I thought of Hansi greeting me inside his tent. 'There is one other small thing,' he said. Then it seemed as if he had become embarrassed, because he started to say that it was nothing, really.

'Hand it over,' Max said.

Bruno reached into his pocket and withdrew a small parcel of tissue paper. He passed it to me and, puzzled, I unwrapped it. There in my hand was a small pebble.

'Jean used to play with that all the time,' Max said. 'She passed it from hand to hand like a favourite toy. She must have left it somewhere – as you can see, it is still smooth, and the blast has hardly touched it. We found it weeks later among the rubble. Does it mean anything to you?'

'Yes.'

Max's gaze did not leave my face.

'She picked it up from beneath the glacier,' I said.

Max nodded, as if he understood everything.

'We kept it for forty years,' Bruno said apologetically, as if he feared that I would accuse him of being absurdly sentimental. 'We didn't have the heart to throw it away.'

'Max,' I asked, 'what are you going to do with it?'

'I don't know. What do you think would be appropriate?' All the time his attention did not leave my face.

I looked down at the pebble. I thought of how she had picked it, and then carried it with her into the heart of a foreign country. And I thought of the wreckage of the house, and of my own image blackening and shrivelling whilst, across the street, Jean's arm rested within dry eaves. My path through life, and my survival, had been achieved only through destruction.

I closed my fist tightly around the pebble, as if my salvation lay within it.

A road had been pushed through the hills to the base of the Versücherin. A coach took us up the valley, past where the deserted farm had been (it had been razed, and a café and gift shop was in its place) and near to the very foot of the wall. An official with a radio cautioned us about the possible danger of falling rocks, and many of us smiled wryly. We were experts, all of us; members of a select band who had climbed the Versücherin wall.

A breeze had risen, and some of the microphones had been sheathed in baffles. A few of our group were agile enough to take a few steps up the face, as if they sought to prove a point, but many of us were too old, or too injured, to find such exertions worth the risk. At a discreet distance there was a police car and an ambulance; it would have been an embarrassment if a member of one of the world's most exclusive clubs were to be taken ill at this moment in this place.

A little further away a helicopter stood on the flattened crest of a hill, its rotor blades turning slowly. I had already been told that it carried oxygen, just in case we had grown unaccustomed to height.

I had long ago ceased to be jealous of those who could still climb such a wall. My hands had lost their dexterity, my body its suppleness, and I had accepted my fate. But I was revered within the group, even though it contained others more courageous, more adventurous than I had ever been.

A television camera moved closer to me, then twisted to take a shot up the wall, its operator adjusting focus as he turned. I was both fascinated by this circus, and uncomfortable within it.

Always there were questions. I told them the route, and I told them about the storm, the frostbite, and how Hansi died. I denied that we had ever talked politics. We had been simple sportsmen, nothing more, who believed that climbing had nothing to do with politics. Max told them how he had been part of the team which had rescued me when I had virtually reached the top. No, he said, there were no photographs; they had all been destroyed by an accident of war. No one mentioned Jean until a young Swiss reporter asked if she was still alive. I shook my head. 'No,' I said, 'she died a long time ago.' The question was not followed up.

The other climbers, too, were asked what they had done, and how they had climbed the face. I had heard of all of these people, but until that day I had met none of them.

Soon we were ushered aboard the helicopter, placed in our seats, and taken up the wall. I found it difficult to adjust to the helicopter's velocity and tilting; the wall was strange and unfamiliar, even though the pilot hovered at certain parts so that we could study it. At such an angle, in such comfort, the wall seemed deceptively simple, even predictable. It held neither treachery nor danger.

We landed near the summit, on a section of cleared ice. A reception committee waited for us, and a man handed out dark glasses, which I took but would not wear. A rubberised tread had been laid between the landing site and the summit so that we could walk easily to the very top of the mountain.

The summit shone with light, and the air was so pure that it caught in my throat. All around me was the whirr of camera motordrives. I walked through the sunlight and the icy air towards the cairn.

The stones had been unpacked from one side of the cairn, leaving a recess. The new logbook had been placed near by on top of a folding pedestal. It was open at the first page so that we, the survivors, could all sign it. I was the first name. There was a scattering of applause when I signed it, and stepped away.

As the others queued up for their turn, I edged my way back to the cairn. When I was sure that no one was looking, I took the pebble from my pocket and placed it within the recess. There was a gap between two of the stones at the bottom of the hollow; I pushed the pebble between them and it vanished. I heard it click as it tumbled and slid within the cairn, then rested at its heart. It would never be found.

Around us, for mile upon mile, the mountains were ranged in an infinity of ridges, and fell into numberless valleys. It was the first time I had seen the view from the top of the Versücherin.